# A CALL TO CHARMS

MAGICAL MIDWAY PARANORMAL COZY SERIES

BOOK SIX

## LEANNE LEEDS

BADCHEN PUBLISHING

A Call to Charms
ISBN Paperback: 978-1-950505-12-8
Published by Badchen Publishing
14125 W State Highway 29
Suite B-203 119
Liberty Hill, TX 78642 USA

For permissions contact: info@badchenpublishing.com

# A CALL TO CHARMS

# CHAPTER 1

THREE WEEKS SINCE GUNTHER BECAME THE ringmaster of the Makepeace Circus. Three weeks. In those three weeks, I saw my boyfriend only twice.

Time spent together?

Ninety-three minutes.

"Look," Fiona said as our girl group sat around the table. "Long-distance relationships *can* work, you know. It's not like you're really in a long-distance relationship, anyway, Charlotte—he's in your *head*. He's about as close in as someone can get."

"Do you even *know* when he's listening in?" Anya asked. She passed a roast chicken across the table toward Fortuna. Her frown made it clear how she felt about Gunther's mental attachment to my thoughts before Fortuna had grabbed the plate. "That would be the end of dating for me. My significant other listening to *everything* I did." The tough-as-nails naiad rolled her eyes and shuddered. "What a nightmare."

"You get used to it," I told her. "He's polite about it. If he listens to something he shouldn't hear, he doesn't mention it."

"Like *that* makes it better," Anya snorted.

"I think it's sweet," Avalon whispered in her breathy voice.

"What? Speak up!" Anya shouted at her. We all jumped. "Can't hear you when you whisper, girlfriend." Anya slapped Avalon on the back and laughed. The skittish weredeer leader winced and glared at her friend.

"How did the two of you *ever* become best friends?" Fiona asked, spooning mashed potatoes onto her plate. "I swear, every time we have one of these get-togethers, it baffles me all the more. I thought I would grow to understand—"

"She's just *lucky*, kelpie," Anya snorted and slapped Avalon on the back again, though more lightly this time. The weredeer shrugged her hand away with a scowl. I thought the two would have it out right at the table as they glowered at one another.

A moment later, though, the corner of Avalon's mouth turned up, and she smiled at the water nymph.

"You don't have to understand it. If you ask me, we sit around far too much trying to understand things around here. Just accept, enjoy, and move on." Anya smiled back. Avalon nodded her agreement.

"If we accept, enjoy, and move on, we'll all be dead by midsummer," Fiona pointed out.

"Before *that*, I suspect," Fortuna chimed in.

Anya didn't disagree, and the table of women grew quiet. It had been a lightheartedly delivered observation, but it was a possibility nonetheless—and we all recognized it. No one wanted to argue. No one wanted to acknowledge the truth.

We were losing.

More than that…we weren't sure what to do to win.

Or what we were *trying* to win.

It was midwinter, and I had been ringmaster of the Magical Midway for a little over a year. It wasn't a position I wanted, but Uncle Phil died and chose me (instead of my father) to take his place—so here we were. I joined the circus at the same moment I became responsible for it, and my father went back to the human world to continue running our family's animal shelter in Mickwac, Texas.

I *missed* Mickwac.

Sure, central Texas summers were brutal. There was always a drought. If there wasn't a drought, there was a flood. I had almost no social life to speak of because I could read everyone's mind and that was…unpleasant. Helping my parents run the family animal shelter could sometimes be depressing. Humans could be so cruel to innocent animals, and that we were a family of witches able to heal the strays that came to us didn't always make it better.

There was a lot about my life there that wasn't perfect.

But still.

I missed it.

I missed living a normal *human* life, the life I had right until the paranormal world sucked me into it by making me the *most powerful witch in the universe.*

Well, one of two, anyway.

*You didn't live a normal human life,* Samson said in my mind. *You were an immature recluse who avoided human contact with almost everybody. The select few you allowed into your personal space didn't do much for you in the maturity department.*

*Shut up.* I blushed.

Samson, my snarky family guardian familiar, wasn't entirely wrong.

But I was doing better. I had a boyfriend. I was taking responsibility.

I had grown up some.

*Some,* Samson snorted.

I ignored the cat and gazed out over the table.

The circus was magical. And I don't mean, like, it was super cool to live in a circus. I mean the thing was *literally* powered by magic and filled with paranormal creatures that most humans thought existed only in myths and fairy tales. Werelions and werebears and weredeers and…well, pick any animal and put *were* on the front of it? We probably had it once, somewhere in our history. That's not even counting the elves, leprechauns, sphinxes…

The paranormals that lived with us and traveled with us? They had become my second family. They rejected the paranormal towns and the rigorous control of the Witches' Council to live a carefree life entertaining humans. A choice that infuriated the Witches' Council with their stringent human/paranormal segregation rules.

Like the human circuses, we popped up in a town and disappeared the next day.

Unlike the human circuses, we teleported to travel.

It was easier.

Before I became the ringmaster, I had thought we were, like, just hippie rejects finding our own way and flying in the face of paranormal convention. Much like our human counterparts, I figured we were a different breed wanting a different life. An adventurous subset of paranormals that lived in traveling circuses to experience life a little differently. No big deal.

That was *not* the case.

We existed because of a powerful goddess-like spirit. For some reason I had yet to understand, she pulled her power back from the world. Since it had to go somewhere, she contained it within the magical circuses. Like we were magical energy Tupperware containers storing the power of transformation on a shelf until *she* decided the world of humans could have it back.

Her godlike husband, Eiggam, did the same. His power of stability animated the goals of the Witches' Council, a group of women that ruled the paranormal world with an iron fist. They demanded obedience from us while also being sworn to destroy the power of transformation held within the circuses.

They *didn't* get our obedience. We refused to let them destroy us.

Well…okay, "us" as in the people I was familiar with.

Like, us at *this* table. Like Gunther and his father.

Some other folks blew off the whole circus commitment thing in exchange for condos in Imperatorial City. Those condos were, of course, courtesy of the Witches' Council Bribery Department. (Okay, okay, there wasn't an actual department named "The Bribery Department." But at the rate they bribed circuses out of existence, maybe there should be.)

Years ago, there were many circuses. Over two dozen existed to hold Maggie's power while she decided what to do with it. His power, Eiggam's? In the hands of the Witches' Council it was used in a two-century long mission to wipe us off the map. The Council had been relentless.

Now, there were only two circuses left.

The Magical Midway, and the Makepeace Circus.

I was in charge of the first.

The man I fell in love with after becoming

ringmaster? He was in charge of the second. And because we were both ringmasters, duty and magical rules seemed designed to ensure that he and I could never be together.

"When is the next Witches' Council meeting, anyway?" Fiona asked between sips of wine. "I feel like every time they schedule one, it gets canceled. Though it shouldn't surprise me at all after the shellacking Mina got when she tried to take over the Makepeace Circus that she canceled the one two weeks ago."

"*That* woman doesn't seem to be able to think on her feet," Anya chuckled.

"They have to have one at some point, don't they?" Fortuna asked.

"I'm thinking they don't *have* to do anything," Fiona told her. Anya and Avalon nodded in agreement. "The rules they cleave to with such a dedication are for everyone else. Not them."

"You might be right," I told them. "They no longer seem to care that everyone can see them breaking their own rules. I think they're kind of making it up as they go along at this point."

"You are assuming anyone is watching," Fiona pointed out. "Or that anyone cares what happens to us. As long as it's not affecting them, I doubt it matters to them."

"Geez, Fiona, that's dark."

Fiona shrugged at me.

"Or they are doing what Eiggam tells them to do." Anya rolled her eyes again. She grabbed the huge wineglass on the table by her plate and threw her head back, draining it with a flourish. When she finished, Anya slammed the chalice back on the table with a satisfied sigh and continued. "Witches following a male god's advice. It would *appall* our ancestors."

"Matriarchal rule didn't work that well, at least if I recall my history." Fortuna reached forward to grab a roll.

"*You* learned human history," Anya scoffed, grabbing a roll before Fortuna's hand made it to the basket and throwing it at her. "Do you think the humans had access to *any* truth about paranormals and who we are? They don't *now*, they didn't *then*, and I can tell you that *my* people grasped well that having women in charge was far better than handing the world over to *men*."

"She's right," Fiona said, nodding.

"I'm surprised to hear *you* say that," Fortuna told her, her eyes wide. The leaders of Fiona's kelpie group were two men, and she was dating Ningul, a male centaur leader. None of us had ever heard Fiona say a cross word about any of them.

"Oh, not about the whole *men should never be in charge* thing." Fiona shook her head. "Ningul is a wise leader of the centaurs, and I have never had a problem with Doug and Kevin—"

"They're gay," Anya cut her off while flapping her hands. "*Not* the same thing. Different culture."

"They're men," Fiona said, pointing. "Gay men, men—"

"*Not* the same thing," Anya insisted, shaking her head.

"I think they would argue with you," Fiona countered.

"Anya has a point, though," Fortuna said. "Gay folks, men or women, have faced discrimination. I think their leadership differs from someone that hasn't. They know what it is to face persecution. People who have faced persecution of any kind understand what it looks like, and they're much more likely to lead with compassion. I think, anyway."

Avalon, Fiona, and Anya stared at Fortuna with their mouths wide open.

"Persecuted? What on *earth* are you talking about?" Anya asked.

"Why would someone be ill-treated for who they date?" Fiona asked in confusion.

Fortuna looked from one to the other, puzzled. Turning, she asked me, "Are they pulling my leg?"

"I don't think the gay thing has the same issues in the paranormal world as it does in the real world—"

"Hey, now!" Anya snapped at me, lurching forward.

"The *human* world," I corrected myself.

"Well, if persecution because of who you date makes someone a better leader, Charlotte must be the greatest leader ever," Fiona chuckled. The other women snickered and nodded.

I smiled and tried not to take it personally.

Since it was probably true.

Well, the part about the persecution.

Not the part about being the greatest leader ever.

I was *not* that.

I strolled through the fairgrounds alone the following morning, my hand busy waving in all directions to mend this and that with magic.

With each mindless step, I thought about everything that had transpired. So much had changed since I became ringmaster a year ago.

I had gained an amazing amount.

And yet I felt I had lost even more.

"Good day to ya, Ringmaster," Hildegaard Brown, the circus's staff chef, greeted me as she lugged a vat along the path. "Pleasant morning for a mending stroll, is it?"

"Hi ya, Hilde. Can I help you get that where it needs to go?" I asked her, waving my hand in a semblance of a magical gesture.

"That would be wonderful, thank ye, ma'am," the brownie said as she lowered the cask with a groan. "Alessandra Atwater's been under the weather of late, and I promised the child I would get her some of my special healing soup. Since she is a naiad, she needs quite a *lot* of liquid, poor dear."

"Oh? Anything I can do?" I asked her. "Anya didn't tell me."

"No, I imagine not, ma'am," Hilde sighed, leaned on the wooden cask like a stool and wiped her brow. "I don't think the girl is ill, not an illness magic could heal. She struggles with guilt, poor thing. Over Dergal, for the things her sister Alexa has done. Things Anya does *not* struggle with, bless her iron heart. The soup will help the naiad," the brownie said. "Only a bit, though. Young Alessandra must work through her heart's cracks on her own."

Guilt bubbled up within me as I realized how little I had paid attention to my people since the prophecy had taken over my life. If Uncle Phil's ghost hadn't stayed around, and if his girlfriend Jeannie hadn't granted his wish to have a body, it's possible this place would have fallen apart.

*You've put your attention where it needed to be,* Samson said, He strolled up and rubbed against Hilde. The brownie's hand snaked into her apron pocket and she dropped a treat on the ground for my guardian familiar. With a polite meow, he swallowed the gift whole and looked up for more.

"Now, Master Samson, you know the rule. Just one per visit or you'll get fat," Hilde scolded him. She leaned down to scratch between Samson's ears. The arrogant cat shook her hand off and trotted away.

*That was rude,* I told him.

*I'm a cat. You remember I'm a cat, right?*

I rolled my eyes.

"I'm used to it." Hilde smiled at me. "It's his nature. We can all only be what we are, Ringmaster."

It was always everyone's nature around here. Seemed to always be an excuse for bad behavior, if you asked me.

People rarely asked me.

"Let me get that cask over to the naiad tent for you," I said, and with a wave of my hand, I transported it to its destination. "There you go."

"Thank you so much," Hilde said as she lifted the hood she always wore and tucked it about her head. "We pride ourselves on our hard work, but I admit, Ringmaster, with my age and arthritis, it's getting harder to lug the vats around of late."

"Is there something I can do?"

"No, no," she waved me off. "Age comes to all of us, *even* magical creatures. Well, *most* magical creatures. That's as it should be, how life *should* work. I accept my lot just fine, ma'am. It's just nice to have a little help now and again." With a smile and a nod, the wrinkly, short woman shuffled off toward the water ride that contained the naiads' hidden home.

A water ride that hadn't run for months now.

There was little to mend at the Magical Midway because it was getting little use as a circus of late. With the Witches' Council determined to destroy us, Ethel Elkins demanding that we follow her every whim and demand, ringmasters getting poisoned...We were nothing more than a traveling campground these days with pretty lights and festive looking tents.

I missed the visiting humans, and I missed the happiness and joy this place could conjure when it did as it was meant to do.

As things became more precarious, I feared allowing humans onto the grounds. Gunther wasn't allowing it, either. It was one thing to put people at risk who had *chosen* this life. It was another to set up, welcome humans onto the grounds, try to show them a good time—all while worrying that the Witches' Council could attack at any moment.

*The one inviolate rule that the Council follows is to never allow humans to know we exist,* Samson said. *They would not risk that even for a chance to take a swipe at you or Gunther.*

*It's not a risk I'm willing to take,* I told Samson. I waved my hand and straightened up the petting zoo. Though no humans had been here, Krog and Oirk's eight goblin children still enjoyed going in the pen and playing. The corral was strewn with toys, balls, and ropes that the children used to yank one another across the dirt.

*Suit yourself,* Samson said. *You are the ringmaster.*

I missed when life was simpler.

Like when Tabitha and I would meet in Austin for chicken-fried steak and talk about boys. Even though Aidan had been a fake boyfriend and even though Tabitha's boyfriend Bobby was a gigantic jerk...the problems I had before I became ringmaster paled in comparison to the concerns I had now.

What does Maggie, the super-powerful being that granted my powers, want from me? Can I trust Ethel Elkins, the old woman so ancient she was alive at the beginning of the fight between Maggie and Eiggam? Does the disagreement between Maggie and Eiggam have to end in a confrontation that would destroy one or the other? Why did Mina side with Eiggam? Why do we have to destroy each other?

*All good questions,* Samson said.

*Yeah, but what are the answers?*

*Isn't your destiny to decide the answers or some such thing?*

*Destiny,* I snorted as I mended the corner of a torn tent. *I feel like I will spend the rest of my life trying to overcome destiny.*

∼

Entering my yurt, I could feel the tension in the room.

Aidan and Kyle talked in the corner as Ethel Elkins shook her hand at them. Devana stood behind the old woman as always. Within a split second of noticing me, the conversation between them stopped. Anger and edginess continued to crackle in the air.

"What now?" I asked the foursome.

"Charlotte, I just—"

"You can't tell her!" Ethel Elkins screeched so loudly that Cama, the death bat, fell off the beam she had been hanging from far above us. "This is a distraction, nothing more, and it has *nothing to do with the prophecy!*"

"If it has nothing to do with your little live-action mystery play, lady, then telling her shouldn't interfere with anything," Kyle told the old woman. The centaur towered over the short woman, who crossed her arms and glared up at him. "She has a right to know, that's why her mother called her—"

"My mother? My mother called? What's wrong?" I asked, panic gripping my insides. My hands felt like ice as potential disasters ran through my mind. "What happened to my parents? Is the shelter okay? My father?"

"Nothing, Charlotte, nothing at all. Your mom and dad are fine, the animal shelter is fine," Aidan told me. He walked toward the spot where I stood. I noticed he was very pale. "The problem is with—"

"Stop it!" Ethel screeched again, stopping him cold. He winced. "I'm telling you, this is a problem we have no time to deal with. Better she not know. You can just let her know when the girl's body is found, she'll go to the funeral, it will take a few hours to mourn, and *done*. Much more simple!" Ethel crossed her arms and harrumphed as she dictated how this would all go. Her angry glare challenged anyone in the room to question her.

"Are you people really so cavalier about death here?" Kyle asked her.

"Not that we're cavalier—" Devana began.

"Don't talk to me." Kyle's head snapped around so he could meet her clear eyes. His penetrating stare paled the dangerous woman. "I need nothing explained to me by a murderer. *Ever*. We clear?" Devana took a deep breath and blinked away the tears that had sprung to her eyes. The elegant woman seemed to shrink where she stood. She nodded and fell silent.

Kyle would not forgive Devana's poisoning of

Roland Makepeace—even if Roland wound up dying of a heart attack later, anyway, and not from the poison. I accepted that it was Roland's time, and that he died so he could be with Gerda, his deceased wife. It took me a while, but I did it. Regardless of all that, though, Devana's actions sowed a deep mistrust in our group and…well, I hadn't *forgiven* her for the attempted murder, either, even if I understood why it all went down the way it did.

"Charlotte, Tabitha—" Aidan started.

"Stop talking!" Ethel Elkins screeched.

"What *about* Tabitha?" I swept Ethel Elkins aside. "What's happened to her? Is she sick?"

"We don't know," Kyle said. He pushed Ethel Elkins aside much more roughly than I had. "We don't know what's happened to her. She's missing. Disappeared two days ago, and it's just now hit the news. Your mom wanted to make sure you were aware."

"This is a *human problem*." Ethel Elkins pushed between the three of us. "You have police officers in the human world, they'll find her, she'll be fine. We have other things we need to worry about."

Aidan glared at Ethel Elkins with undisguised disgust.

Tabitha, my best friend from the human world, was missing.

She was in trouble.

Without saying a word, I raced out of the yurt toward the edge of the fairgrounds. It was time to teleport the Magical Midway to Mickwac, Texas. And I didn't want to hear a single thing about it from Ethel Elkins.

# CHAPTER 2

"Did she say anything else?" I asked Aidan as we hiked up the path toward my childhood home. "Do the police have any idea what might have happened to her? Did you get the gist of anything other than that she's missing?"

"No, Charlotte, you're aware of everything that your mom told me." Aidan raced behind me. I took the steps to the porch two at a time. "I wish I had asked more questions, but I wanted to get you so we didn't chat long."

"I can reach out to my contacts in the police department. Just, um…" Kyle slapped against all of his pockets looking for the cell phone he no longer carried since he moved to the Magical Midway. He looked up at me. "I need a phone."

"Follow me. My mom still has a landline in the kitchen." I swung the back door open with a yank. "You can call whoever you need from there."

My nose filled with the scent of my childhood as we walked in off the back deck. The flowery scent of my mother's cleaner mixed with the fading aroma of freshly baked bread. Nothing had changed. The same Formica table with its chipped corner held the center of the room, chairs slightly pulled out to welcome anyone that entered.

"Charlotte! I guessed you would be here soon." My mother came in from the living room and held out her arms. We hugged briefly, but I pulled back to scrutinize her expression. It was grave. "Your father is out in the back, taking care of the dogs, but he'll be back up here in a few minutes. Can I get any of you anything to eat? Drink? I can whip up eggs, or—"

"No, Mom, thanks," I said as her hand made for the cast-iron skillet on the stove. "We're good. Not hungry, just worried."

"Aidan, it's good to see you." My concerned mother stretched her hand out for my friend and pulled him in for a hug. "The circus life agrees with you; you look good."

"Thanks, Mrs. Astley." Aidan smiled at her briefly. "I'm surprised. The circus has been a bit of a demanding thing of late."

"I'm sure that all of you together can handle whatever comes your way," my mother insisted. She pulled the chairs out even further from the kitchen table and waved to Aidan and Kyle to sit down.

"Actually, Mrs. Astley, if I can use your phone? I want to put a call in to some cops I was close to and see if I can find out any information beyond what you saw on the news," Kyle said. My mother went to the side of the kitchen and held up a rotary phone that looked like it should've been replaced in the seventies. "Thanks, I appreciate it."

"Is there anything else I can do for any of you?" Mom asked.

*Do you need me to come?* Gunther's voice burst through my mind. For a split second, anger flared within me that Gunther had been riding shotgun on my perceptions without notifying me, but that faded instantly. I was thankful that I didn't have to explain what was going on.

*I wish you were here, if that's what you're asking,* I said telepathically. With Samson required to stay on the Magical Midway, and the barrier that sheltered the Midway blocking any connection with him, I was alone in my head, mostly. Even though Gunther could communicate with me through the lawgiver bond, it wasn't as reassuring as having him here. *I don't have any idea about anything at the moment. We just got here. I'll contact you after Kyle gets an update directly from the police.*

"Okay, so what *exactly* did the news say, Mom? I rushed out to move us without getting much more than the fact that she's missing." I leaned up against the counter. Mom pulled out a chair for me, but I shook my head. Mom reached for my shoulder gently and nodded.

"Two days ago, Tabitha was driving home from her parents house after having dinner. Her car was found on Old Mill Road—"

"That makes no sense. Well, not if she lives where she used to," I cut my mother off and looked at Aidan. "You lived here far longer than I did. Does that make any sense to you, Aidan? Did she move?"

Aidan shook his head no. "When I lived here, she lived in the same apartment. As far as I can *read*?" His eyes glowed with his magical ability to read the strands of the past. "I think she still lives in the same apartment. The one near the campus, in between her parents' place and downtown.

Since none of us have seen her recently, though, keep in mind I might be mistaken."

"Old Mill Road is *completely* out of the way. What on earth would she be doing there?" I turned toward the stack of maps that leaned against the wall. With so many animals coming from so many directions and Internet maps often getting confused in rural Texas about street names, my parents kept a significant paper map collection. I plucked the one for the small suburb of Strongfair just outside of Austin and spread it out on the kitchen table.

"So, this is where her apartment is," I pointed and glanced around for something to mark the spot. My mother wiggled her hand, and an X appeared. "Right. Thanks, Mom. Okay, and over here is where her parents' house is." With another hand wiggle, another X appeared. "Do we have any idea where on Old Mill Road her car was discovered?"

"At the crossing right by the creek," my mother responded and she wiggled her hand for a final time. "The car was actually parked on the overpass that went over the water."

"Parked on the overpass?" I mumbled as my brow creased. The creek on Old Mill Road was a shallow one filled with rocks. A lot of the time, it wasn't even a creek. It was just a fissure where the water run-off would go if it rained heavily.

Years ago, after multiple days of heavy rain, Tabitha and I had once tried to paddle it—but we wound up lugging our inflatable canoes along the banks more than we floated through the water that looped around the state park. The road itself was just two lanes, an old country road with no lights and no real purpose other than to connect the country folk that lived in that area to the main highway along the back of the park. "That bridge is ridiculously narrow. No one would just park on that bridge. It's too dangerous."

"Well, that's what the police are claiming," Kyle said as he walked in and hung up the wall phone. "Her car was found pristine, locked up tight as if she left all her things in it and walked away. No blood, no broken glass, nothing. At first, they assumed she jumped into the creek."

"No way!" I insisted angrily. "There's no way Tabitha would kill herself! Besides, that bridge isn't even that high."

"I agree, that's an absurd idea," Aidan said.

"More often than not, a car on a bridge means someone tried to off themselves, so that's what they went with. A search of the creek below turned up nothing. If she had jumped, there would've been evidence, so I don't think that's what happened. Mike Lambert said there was nothing at all in the area to show anything else, either, though." Kyle tapped the X over the creek crossing. "The creek itself is muddy but there were no footprints. No footprints on either side of the bridge, either. Her purse and her keys were in the car. Power was off, the car was in park, emergency brake was on. No one saw her walking on the long road in either direction."

"So it's like she locked everything up and walked away," I mumbled again to no one in particular while staring at the map. "But there's nothing out there. Nothing but ranches and farms. She would've had to drive fifteen miles out of her way just to *get* there. And why would she leave her keys in the car? Or her purse?"

"If I remember correctly," Kyle said. "That's a dead zone for cell phones, too. If she got in trouble? She wouldn't have been able to call for help."

"Was there anything wrong with the car?" I asked him. He shook his head no.

"When the police took it in and examined it, it looked fine. They put the key in and started it up at the lab, and there was nothing wrong with it. There is no reason that Tabitha couldn't have driven home in that car," Kyle said. "It had half a tank of gas, the battery was good, it functioned perfectly."

"How about her cell phone?" I asked him.

"In the car with her keys, inside her purse. It's secured by her fingerprint," Kyle said. "The cops are having a hard time getting in. They'll probably have to go to court and get the company to breach the security. Which they may or may not do."

"I'm sure we could get in," I told him standing up.

"You mean with…" Kyle wiggled his fingers to mimic a magical flourish. What he wound up doing was looking like a spasmodic drunk that had just been stung by bees all over his hands.

"Well, I was planning on doing it more gracefully than you, but yes. Magic should be able to unlock the phone," I told him. "There's got to be away for me to turn my hand into a copy of hers. At least one good enough to fool the cell phone sensor."

"Even if we could do that, *how* are we going to justify it? They already know there's no way to get in the phone by code."

"And how are you going to get the phone? Isn't it in evidence or something at the police station? Kyle isn't a detective anymore." My mother shook the water off a mug and placed it in the dish tray. "I can't believe the police will let you walk in there and handle evidence."

"Probably not," I agreed. "Ugh, I wish Gunther were here. He's so much better at this regular magic stuff than I am."

*No problem, love,* Gunther's voice echoed through my brain. *Give me about twenty minutes and we'll be parked next to you in no time.*

*No, Gunther, you don't have to...Gunther? Gunther!*

He hung up on me.

"His magic will incorporate covering his arrival the same as yours, I'm sure?" my father asked me nervously. We stood on the porch gazing out over the field behind the house.

"I don't know, I never asked, but I would assume so," I answered.

"Two circuses suddenly showing up will look suspicious, Charlotte," my father said. His hands were working his fingers back and forth. It was a nervous habit of his but one I had seldom seen. I knew he was right about the two circuses causing suspicion, but there wasn't anything I could do about it before Gunther arrived. If he could hear me in his head because of the lawgiver bond, he was ignoring me. "The two of you don't seem to think twice about taking risks."

"Oh, we *think* twice." I grabbed his hand and squeezed. "There just always seems to be some big, perilous problem that winds up being worth the risk."

Dad's nervous face turned to look at me, and his expression changed to one of concern. Nodding, he wrapped his arms around me and gave me a fatherly hug, kissing my forehead like he used to do when I was a girl. With a start, I realized Gunther kissed me the same way—especially before he became ringmaster and my super strength could crush him like a bug.

"You're right, I'm sorry, I realize you're very concerned for your friend. And you're right to be," my father released me and turned his face back to the field to continue examining the horizon. "I always liked that girl. It was a shame you fell out with one another."

"We didn't *fall out* with one another, Dad," I said. "I lied to her for months. She couldn't trust me after she found out that Aidan and I were faking a relationship just to get her off our backs. Dishonesty is her pet peeve. She can't stand it."

"Well, most people don't like to be lied to, honey."

"Yeah, and I know I shouldn't have done it. I didn't think at the time…I mean, with her wedding to Bobby and everything, I thought I was solving a problem for her. You know, giving her one less thing to worry about."

"Over there," my father pointed as the Makepeace Circus shimmered onto the dusty Texas field. The two circuses next to each other drastically contrasted. The Magical Midway circus presented as a vintage step into the past, a reminder of an era mostly long gone.

The Makepeace Circus was shiny and stylish with fancy rides and electric signs, a modern amusement park in every way other than a static locale.

We embraced and celebrated our tie to the past. Gunther's circus blended in to the present and gave hints of the future.

"Well, that's certainly a sight," my father murmured, taking in the two enormous fairgrounds.

"Naw, that's the sight I'm waiting for," I told Dad. I pointed toward Gunther emerging from the Makepeace Circus gate. He raised his hand and waved. I waved back and tried to launch myself off the porch magically like a comet streaking across the sky.

Okay, not really.

But it felt like it.

"Charlotte, don't forget…The two of you need to make the circuses less conspicuous. You're about to go poking around in the police investigation of your missing friend," my father called after me as I raced down the steps. "Let's not give the humans a reason to be even more suspicious of us."

"I will," I called over my shoulder.

"You will what?" Gunther shouted from the tree-lined path. His smile lit up his face and his sandy blond hair blew gently in the Texas wind.

"Give you a great big hug!" I called back, smiling. My feet picked up the pace toward Gunther without my consciously thinking about it. I had missed him so much. When he was gone, it was like a tooth had been pulled that I kept checking for. I was always surprised that it was gone.

"I'm like a tooth, am I?" Gunther laughed when we met along the path. I embraced him gently, careful to restrain my eagerness. I didn't want to crush him with my super strength. He laughed in reply and wrapped his arms around me, crushing me tight. "You can't injure me or snap my bones anymore, Charlotte, so you better give me a proper hug!"

As we clanged together, I realized that Gunther, too, was protected by ringmaster protections. The two of us sounded like armored knights clashing together, the encasement that protected both of us invisible to the eye but not to the ear. I relaxed into his embrace, snuggling into him without my usual delicate care.

Burying my head in his neck, I breathed in deeply. Hay, and the liniment the Makepeace Circus used on the werehorses, and leather, and musk...the distinct incense of Gunther.

As Gunther and I made our way up to the main house behind the animal shelter, we raised our eyes to the porch to find *all four* of our parents staring down at us with loving expressions. The ghosts of Roland and Gerda Makepeace shimmered next to my flesh and blood parents.

Oh, jeez.

All eight eyes were slightly misty.

"The first one of you that asks when you will get grandchildren will be banished from the midways," I told the four. We climbed up the stairs and Gunther's face beamed with happiness as his mother moved toward him.

"That wasn't my question at all," Roland Makepeace barked from behind Gerda. "Why would any of us ask that question when the two of you can't be together, and even if you could, you can't—"

"Roland!" Gerda scolded and her head snapped back. Although Gerda was a ghost, I could swear I saw a muscle in her jaw twitch. Her eyes blazed at her husband.

"What? We're all thinking it," he grumbled.

"It's good to see you, too, Dad." Gunther smiled as we reached the top step and climbed onto the porch. "After I overheard the conversation you had with Charlotte in the security building, I thought death might've softened you. Good to see things haven't changed."

"Hogwash!" Roland shouted, his eyes burning with indignation.

"Roland, let up on the boy, he's just arrived," Gerda told her gruff husband. She leaned forward and placed a ghostly kiss on Gunther's forehead. "Son, it's so good to see your face. It's just unfortunate it's in these circumstances."

"It's always in these circumstances, Mom," Gunther told her with a sad smile. "Where's my new little sister?"

With a pop, little Anna manifested in the center of the entire group. Her arms outstretched and her legs planted wide, she looked like she had just concluded a vaudeville performance. "Here I am!" she shouted. Squealing, she levitated toward Gunther and wrapped her little arms around his neck. "My brother is here! My brother's here!"

"Are you staying out of trouble, Anna?" Gunther asked. The little girl turned his breath frosty.

"Not really, no," she shook her head. "Only sometimes. When I'm too tired."

Gunther laughed and she floated back down to the porch.

"Gunther, it's good to see you, young man." My father extended his hand formally to my boyfriend. At least, I guess he's still my boyfriend…

*It looks like I arrived just in time for many reasons,* Gunther thought as he overheard my slightly brooding apprehension about our

relationship. *That you could even question that...
What am I going to do with you?*

I blushed.

"You, too, sir," Gunther pumped my father's
hand and nodded respectfully toward my mother.
"Ms. Astley."

"Gunther, it's wonderful to see you.
Congratulations on your recent elevation. I'm
sure you will do your illustrious family honor in
your role," my mother said and bowed her head
with respect. Roland Makepeace beamed with
pride. My father rolled his eyes.

"Yes, yes, what she said," Dad added hastily. "I
hate to end the friendly greetings and formalities,
but two gigantic circuses to the west of our
animal shelter? It will draw attention," he
explained, his forehead creasing. "I appreciate
that we have an emergency here, and Charlotte is
grateful for your help, young Gunther, but—"

"No need to say any more, Mr. Astley,"
Gunther said. His jaw tightened. Closing his eyes,
he flicked his hand and the Makepeace Circus
shimmered.

Then it disappeared.

My jaw dropped.

"How the heck did you *do* that?" I asked. My
eyes searched the now empty field. Not a bush

was disturbed, no dust danced on the air. It was as if the Makepeace Circus had never been there at all.

"Magic." Gunther opened his eyes. I glared at him, and he shrugged, but his eyes sparkled mischievously. I could feel the joy he got from surprising me pouring off of him.

I turned away and continued my slack-jawed stare at the space. "Tell me how you did that! Are they still there?"

"They are, sort of," Gunther said as he pointed. "Remember that place we go when we're elevated to ringmaster?" I nodded. During the elevation ceremony after my uncle passed away, something transported the entire circus to this dark void of a place. I didn't know where it was, but I knew from what my uncle had said that it wasn't likely a place on earth. "Well, it's sort of a reality just for us. Like an alternate dimension only accessible to ringmasters. Something created it to be a place of protection when the power passes from one person to another. Turns out it doesn't just go away, and we can use it for other things."

"So, you sent them there to that black place?" I shuddered recalling the void. There was no light, no stars...It was just an odd expanse of...well, nothing. I couldn't wait to get out of there and frankly, I never wanted to go back.

"Well, it's not black *anymore*," he told me with a half smile. "I redecorated a little. I'm kind of surprised no one did before, actually. Not that hard." Gunther shrugged.

"The ringmaster power? I mean, you did that with the ringmaster power, right?" I asked him.

"Sort of," Gunther's brows drew together. "I used regular magic to tether it to the ringmaster power so I would have most of my abilities when I go off the grounds. The further away I get, the less powerful I am, but we're close right now to where the Makepeace Circus is anchored to the land, so I'm almost at full power."

"I...you're...wow," I blanched as the sheer immensity of what Gunther could figure out and change in just a few short weeks overwhelmed me. For a year, my power had mostly ended at the edge of the fairgrounds. Beyond our circus, something protected me, but I was not magically powerful. Magically, I had only my own skills to protect me, and my witch skills were marginal.

It's not like it was *my* fault. My father wanted to ensure I lived in the human world and not the paranormal one, so he never taught me magic as I was growing up.

Yeah, I know.

It didn't work out the way he'd hoped.

Anyway, Gunther had found a way around that.

*In a few weeks.*

It made me feel like a failure of a ringmaster, to be honest. I stared at the floor, embarrassed at how little I had done and how much better than me Gunther was at the whole ringmaster gig. He had methodically attacked issues that had been plaguing ringmasters and found solutions for them.

*In a few weeks.*

While I…well, I could mend barrels like a champ.

"None of that," Gunther said, putting his hands on my shoulders. I continued staring at my shoes, blinking back tears of embarrassment while our families looked on.

*Charlotte.*

Gunther's gentle hands snaked up to my neck and lifted my chin so he could stare into my eyes. "You had no motivation to tear apart the limits of the power. You had no reason to test what you could do, so you never did so. It's just that simple. If you *had* done so, I *know* you would have found some of these solutions the same as I did."

I rolled my eyes as he placated me.

"Oh, please. I appreciate you trying to make me feel like less of a failure, but I never even tried any of this. I mean, what special motivation did you have to tear these things apart and figure out how they worked?" I asked.

"*You*, Charlotte," Gunther told me. Sadness overtook his features. "My motivation was *you* and finding a way for *us*. Two circuses with two ringmasters that love each other. That want to move forward. *Together*."

I blushed.

"You're working so hard on saving the world, so I figured I could work on this while we're apart." He leaned forward and gently kissed me. "Which we won't be for long. I'm pretty determined, so don't be surprised if I come up with a solution. Besides," a shadow passed over his face, "I had to find something to pass the time."

"As long as it doesn't involve a prophecy, I'm all for it," I told him.

Roland Makepeace's chest puffed up again with pride.

# CHAPTER 3

"WE SHOULD GO TO HER PARENTS' HOUSE FIRST," Aidan said as we stared at the map. "It'd be a kindness to see if they need anything, anyway. Her mother is probably coming apart at the seams, and they don't have a lot of family in the area."

"Does Tabitha have any siblings? Likely it would be better to speak to them instead." My mother dried her always busy hands on her smock for the tenth time since we arrived. "If you were missing, Charlotte, I wouldn't be...well—" Her voice trailed off, and I perceived an empathetic wave of pain flare from her.

"I know, Mom."

Our eyes met, and for just a second I had a

peek into the deep well of worry and apprehension that my mother had for me as ringmaster of the Magical Midway. Tabitha's disappearance had poked many of her fears about me, an uneasiness she worked to bury deep within her. The well was now overflowing, and her frantic cleaning was the only way she could deal with the rising dread.

"I realize you know, sweetheart," Mom smiled weakly. My mother's particular talent was being able to calm and soothe and stimulate the emotions of those around her. Unfortunately, she couldn't turn her power on herself. I reached out and squeezed her hand. She nodded and pulled her hand away, waving at me to continue.

"Tabitha's an only child. No siblings. So we'll have to stop by and see her parents first." The energy from my mother fired up and tamped down like sparks off bellows-fed fire. Her hands continue to twist against the apron, drying skin that was no longer damp. It saddened me how Tabitha's disappearance had shaken her, but there was nothing I could do about it right now.

"You're taking this remarkably well, girl, considering the danger that your friend is in," Roland complimented me with an attempt at a hearty slap on the back, but due to his spectral status his palm simply flew through me. With a sheepish shrug, he continued. "Or *was* in. Have you thought about using that bat to make sure that the human isn't dead? Wouldn't want to waste time poking around when it wasn't needed and there's nothing to be done."

I didn't want to ask Cama, the death bat, whether Tabitha was still alive. It made sense from an informational point of view, but Roland's suggestion hit the bulls-eye of my deepest fear. I wasn't ready to entertain the idea that something terrible had happened to my friend, and it irritated me that Roland went there so hastily before we had even gone to look for her.

Gerda and Gunther admonished Roland harshly for his flippant observation as the blood drained from my face. The rotund ghost shrugged and rolled his eyes, silently communicating his impatience. "While I understand this would be a sad thing, we have other issues we have to focus on," Roland explained. "I don't *want* the poor girl to be dead, but in the human world, when people disappear that *is* most often the situation, is it not? Policeman? You there! Aren't I correct?"

Roland turned to Kyle, Aidan's boyfriend and the latest paranormal to join our circus. Well, if you didn't count the death bat. They kind of joined at the same time, actually. Kyle hadn't known that he was a centaur, and he lived life as a human—until the point he set foot on the Magical Midway and the circus flexed its might and right to claim another hidden paranormal.

Once his energy mixed with our energy…well, that was all she wrote for Detective Kyle. Half man, half horse, *wholly* confused.

He was handy to have around though. As I waited for his professional judgment, I wondered how he would react to being back in Mickwac.

"Not really," Kyle told Roland, who rolled his eyes again. "Some individuals disappear and are found months or years later perfectly fine. If Tabitha was a missing child, the situation would be different—but she's an adult. We don't know that her disappearance at this point is involuntary, much less that there's been some kind of foul play."

"She's alive," I said to Roland.

"You hope," Roland told me as he leaned forward and stared into my eyes. "You *have* a death bat, Charlotte. You may as well ask Cama for help! What's the point of being a paranormal if we will not use the magic at our disposal? It's ridiculous! Stop thinking like a human, girl, and think like a witch!"

The group grew quiet as Gunther's father barked orders at me.

It's a quiet I was intimately familiar with. It's the quiet that settles upon a meeting when everyone is afraid to speak, or no one has any ideas, or when what's facing us is too difficult to contemplate. Or...when everyone concurs. When no one spoke up for me, I knew that while the group wasn't happy with the way Roland spoke to me, the assembled group felt he *had* a point.

*He means well, Charlotte,* Gunther thought. I continued to stare at his father, breathing fear in and out of my lungs for my friend. *When people go missing from the circuses, it's almost always been that someone has killed them in the outside world. My father—*

*Is the most insensitive person I've ever met.*

Gunther didn't respond to my observation about his father. I assumed that was because he had no quarrel to make with *that* point, either.

The screen door off the kitchen creaked, and my father entered the room. Wasn't he here with us the whole time? Fear for Tabitha, indignation at Roland, and the Texas heat I was no longer accustomed to gripped me. I looked around to take stock of who was in the room, but white spots appeared before my eyes. My stomach lurched wildly as the image of Tabitha shouting flashed in my mind.

"Charlotte, are you all right?" Gunther asked as he approached me.

"It's too hot, and…and I am…feeling a little… Kyle, did you call your friend at the precinct?" I asked Aidan's centaur boyfriend. Blinking quickly, I tried to clear Tabitha's face from my gaze.

My throat suddenly felt like it was on fire, and I gulped at the air.

"What's wrong with her?" my mother asked, her voice low. "Her color looks odd."

"I don't know, she's wobbling on her feet—"

"Gunther!" my father cried.

"I have her!" he called back and folded his arms around me.

"Hey, handsome," I laughed drunkenly as I fell into his arms. The clang of our psychic armor crashing together echoed through my skull, and I grimaced. I leaned my head against him. "I can't… see you…through the stars…it surrounds Tabitha…by stars glistening…"

"What is she talking about? What's happening to her?"

I heard my mother call, but her voice sounded far away. Chairs scraped against the kitchen floor, boots echoed through the crawlspace below. Somewhere far away, a dog barked. It felt as though there were many hands on me, and my feet separated from the floor.

"Charlotte!" my mother shouted.

"Oh, Mom, it'll be fine…I'm sure I'm fine…" I slurred as the darkness swallowed me.

"She should go back to the Magical Midway," Ethel Elkins demanded with an earsplitting shriek. While I slowly crawled back to awareness, Ethel Elkins screaming about something or another wasn't exactly the sound I wanted to greet me. "Taking a side trip into the human world to chase after one lowly mortal is a preposterous misuse of her time, and now it's made her ill," Ms. Elkins continued. I opened my eyes to find myself lying on the couch in my parents' living room. Gunther kneeled beside me, his face concerned.

"I'm fine," I mumbled and forced myself up. "I passed out. No big deal."

"People don't *just faint*, Charlotte,." Gunther

helped me sit up. My mom handed me a glass of ice water over Gunther's shoulder, and I gulped it down gratefully.

"I think she should see a doctor," my father said with concern.

"A human doctor? Are you demented?" Ethel Elkins scoffed.

"I have healing skills," Devana said unassumingly. She stepped out from behind the short, fat old woman. She bowed her head, hands clasped demurely in front of her. "I would be happy to look at Charlotte and ensure that she is healthy. With her approval."

"You stay away from her," Kyle snapped at the huntress witch. With two determined steps, he moved rapidly to take up space between me and Devana. The quiet woman raised her chin and gazed at the angry ex-cop. A muscle in Devana's jaw twitched, but other than that she had no reply.

"You centaurs are consistently so overly theatrical," Ethel Elkins snapped back. She stepped up to Kyle and stabbed him with a plump finger in the gut. I think she probably wanted to poke him in the chest but she was too small to reach. "You're all standing here gawking at Charlotte! What could Devana possibly do to a ringmaster? Much less with all of you people gaping at her?"

"So all it would've taken was my staring at my father, and she wouldn't have poisoned him?" Gunther asked tightly. I reached out and placed my hand on his arm but he didn't turn his head.

"Son, let's not bring that up," Roland's ghost swept away Gunther's concern with a wave of his hand. "The huntress witch was accomplishing something required. We spoke about that. She meant well."

"I don't know when murder ever means well, Dad."

"Hey, could we refocus, please?" I demanded. I leaned forward on the couch and set the ice water down on the coffee table. "Maybe instead of all of you choosing for me, I could get a vote here?"

"You decide for all of us all the time, Charlotte," Roland Makepeace said with a playful smirk. "It seems only fair we turn the tables on you when you're weakened. I mean, how often do we get the chance, honestly?"

"Thanks so much for that, Mr. Makepeace," I rolled my eyes.

"Charlotte, I think you should go to a real doctor," my father insisted again.

"Look, Dad…If I go to an everyday human

physician, and they try to take blood, the needle will snap in two. If he or she tries to look down my throat with a tongue depressor, it may snap into splinters. With the ringmaster protection rendering me a virtually impenetrable clanging mass of invisible metal, I don't think going to human doctor is such a good idea."

My father's face fell. He had overlooked just how powerful and conspicuous the force field around me was.

"Alan, she's correct," my mom told him. "She requires a paranormal healer."

"And she can't go to the Witches' Hospital in Impy," Gunther pointed out.

"Look, you guys, I'm fine now. This is all getting ridiculous—"

"No, she can't," my father said. "Gunther, don't you have reparative powers as a ringmaster? Charlotte told me you mended that girl's back. Hayden's sister, wasn't it?"

"Healing powers, yes," Gunther nodded. "If there's an injury to bones, nerves, I can mend it. *Diagnostic* powers, no. Diagnosing someone's illness, whether physical or paranormal, is still a learned skill and if it doesn't involve something out of place from where it should be, I don't have that skill. I can heal the obvious, but we still use our own healer at the Makepeace Circus."

"Well, let's get the healer," Kyle said.

"We have to bring back the Makepeace Circus to Mickwac, and I think Charlotte's father is right. Two circuses? Someone will notice. It's just not normal to have two different circuses set up side-by-side. I can't pull one person out of the void."

I understood my father's concern regarding passing humans' confusion at seeing two circuses set up in the field next to the animal shelter. But...I had to admit I was becoming increasingly frustrated. So far, we debated who should check me out after I blacked out, debated two circuses sitting side-by-side and whether that would be a concern.

And while all this was going on, Tabitha was missing.

"Devana will check me out," I told the group and pulled myself to a sitting position. "We're not gonna bring back the Makepeace Circus. Once Devana pronounces me healthy and A-okay, we're going to Tabitha's parents' house. That's what will happen. That's the way it will be. Until we find Tabitha, the human world is our priority. She's our priority."

"But Charlotte—"

"Gunther, I realize that you're concerned about me. But I'm here, and I'm breathing. Until I know for sure where Tabitha is and that she's—" I couldn't say the word breathing. I still couldn't contemplate the thought something so terrible had happened to Tabitha that she might be...dead.

"Charlotte won't be all right until we know that Tabitha is," Aidan said. I gulped down the knot in my throat and nodded.

"Let's go up to my old room and you can check me out there," I said to Devana and headed toward the stairs. I needed to get away from all the eyes on me, and all the squabbling. "You hang here."

"Who, me?" Ethel Elkins asked.

"Yes," I responded. "And if anyone else wants to ask whether I mean them, I do. All of you, stay here."

"Charlotte, let me come with you." Gunther tried to follow. His glance at Devana made clear his concern.

"Gunther, it's fine," I told him and turned back. "We will be right upstairs." Turning away, I continued my climb up the stairs. Devana followed me silently. The eyes of my family and friends stared at her skeptically. I peeked back one last time at Gunther and caught him watching me, his pale eyes hurt. He felt rejected, I could tell. And it wounded him.

I didn't feel guilty. Maybe I should have, but I didn't.

"You obviously made no friends around here," I told Devana as we reached the landing. Pointing toward the closed door at the end of the hall, I added. "Though I blame Ethel Elkins more than I blame you."

"Perhaps I will earn back their faith," Devana answered. "I thank you for allowing me to earn back yours."

"You *haven't* earned back my confidence." We came face-to-face outside my childhood bedroom door. "But you are a huntress and you stalk prey. I may need you here in a few hours. Tabitha's been missing for two days. Roland was right about one thing; I owe it to her to use whatever tools are at my disposal to find her. That includes you."

"I will assist in any way I can, Ringmaster," Devana said. Her eyes blazed with determination as she met my gaze. "I do not wish to be your enemy."

"Then stop trying to kill my friends," I told her. "That would be a good start."

She sighed and we walked into the bedroom.

"I can find nothing physically wrong with you, Charlotte," Devana said while I slipped my shirt back on. "I did not expect that anything other than poison could physically harm a ringmaster, but I scanned for absolutely any physical problem. You have none. You are perfectly healthy. Healthier than most witches, in fact."

"Any ideas why I fainted?" I asked her.

"It could have been a magical attack," Devana said thoughtfully. "A psychic attack, perhaps. Because you repelled it, the energy is no longer around you. I can no longer examine what is past."

"If someone attacked me, Aidan could tell me, couldn't he?"

"The past-reader has access to things that people understand. His abilities and their strengths depend on the people he comes into contact with, and things *they* mean him to know," Devana explained. "If you and I don't know what just happened to you, and he has not recently seen the person that attacked you, he may not read what just occurred."

"Is there a single person that has a power that doesn't come with limitations, addenda, codicils and postscripts?" I asked her in exasperation, not expecting an answer. Sunlight streamed in from the window behind her. It bathed her in an almost otherworldly glow.

"There is a balance in all things," Devana responded sagely. "Unfettered power is dangerous."

"But there's not balance in all things, right? If there *was*, it would balance everything and be perfect and nobody would fight," I told her. I sat down on my childhood bed. Okay, it wasn't just my childhood bed. It was the bed I slept in until I was in my thirties, but let's ignore that for a second and call it my childhood bed.

"Balance is a *goal*, Charlotte, an ideal we strive for. It is the center we rotate around, and a force that keeps us from making too great a mess of things. Balance does not create a utopia or make evil disappear."

"What does?" I asked her.

"Well, nothing does," Devana responded. She pulled the chair from under my study desk and sat down daintily. Everything about Devana was elegant. I felt like a clod next to her. She moved with such incredible grace, and I…well, I didn't. When I met her at the Werebear Jamboree, I felt instinctively that I could trust her even though nothing she specifically said *told* me I could.

But then she poisoned Roland Makepeace, and the instinctive trust I had in her shattered.

"You don't understand why I do what I do," Devana said after I didn't respond. It was more of a statement than a question.

I didn't want to have this conversation.

Tabitha was missing, and every moment that passed could be a moment where her fate sealed. Time was of the essence and dealing with the prophecy wasn't high on my list. Devana *was* a Huntress, though. The huntress witches were renowned for being able to find and catch anything they sought. It was likely I would need her help to find Tabitha.

Yet…I did not understand her. I didn't know if I could trust the woman.

"It's more than that," I told her, leaning back against my headboard with a clang. "Your actions, your willingness to *kill* someone because you thought it was right…You make me wonder whether *we* are on the right side of the fight."

"We are, of course we are," she insisted as the

blood drained from her face. Her lower lip trembled as she considered me. "How could you even question that? You, of all people?"

"I don't see a difference between you poisoning Roland Makepeace because you believed it was time for him to die and the Witches' Council sending someone to kill the leader of the werebears because it would serve their purposes to have a different leader," I said. "Our side and their side have *both* killed to suit their purposes. I can't see that as anything other than evil. I don't understand how you can."

Devana cast her eyes downward and her face flushed. "You believe I am evil?"

"You didn't do what you did alone," I admitted. "You did it as a representative of my side, so if you're evil, so am I."

"Charlotte, you cannot think such a thing. Surely, you don't believe that."

"I don't know what I believe right now, to tell you the truth," I told her. She lifted her eyes and the two of us stared at one another. I could see the things I said pained her, but I couldn't find it in myself to feel guilty about that, either, any more than I felt guilty about hurting Gunther. She tried to *kill* someone. She *should* feel pain over that. "I know that I don't have time to think about it."

"Yes, we must find your friend," Devana nodded and stood up, relieved the subject we were discussing changed. The huntress witch walked toward the bedroom door, her hands clasped in front of her tightly. After a moment, she stopped and turned to face me. "I am sincerely sorry that my choice not to speak to you on my own has led to such doubts in you. I suspected that Ms. Elkins would not explain our actions so you would understand."

"She didn't explain them at all." Devana stared at me and then nodded.

"I understand your wariness, and your mistrust of me," Devana smiled sadly. "I once told you I could not do other than what Ethel Elkins demanded of me to make up for the sin of my people."

"You did. I didn't understand how Mina's choice somehow bound you to Ethel Elkins' demands then, and I don't understand it now. I don't believe her sin is on you. That's on her."

Mina World, the head of the Witches' Council, was responsible for the fight between Eiggam and Maggie, the two godlike powers at the center of the paranormal divisions. Mina sided with Eiggam, the god in charge of preservation, of things that do not change. The circuses contained Maggie's power of change and transformation. It locked the two powers in a battle for supremacy.

The old ways would be preserved and controlled with Mina ruling over the paranormal world as if it were her personal dictatorship, or we would...what?

I didn't know. I knew I was the thirteenth witch, and I would have to make a choice. But I didn't know what that choice was, or why it fell to me to make it.

"There are many things you don't understand yet, and I am sorry for that," Devana said. She looked troubled, and that made me nervous. "I am unsure about what I understand sometimes and I...I fear saying anything in case my misunderstanding would change things irrevocably. I don't wish to damage our fight. There is one thing I am sure enough of, though, Charlotte—I think you will make the most progress in your understanding when you step out of the shadow of all those elders who demand of you."

"What does that mean?" I crossed my arms. "And why the sudden change? You've been demanding that I listen to Elkins with the same unwavering loyalty you do."

"Perhaps I was wrong," Devana replied. Heat stained her cheeks. It was clear the huntress witch was not accustomed to being wrong. "Wisdom really must be earned, Charlotte. That is not some trick, or some saying the surrounding people are telling you to keep you ignorant of your true path. The key to your success is in the earning. Mina is what you get when someone does not earn their wisdom."

I covered my eyes with my hand and rubbed my eyeballs. These paranormals and their lectures about ethics and morality. They could seriously give me a headache. Devana chuckled softly as I sighed.

"If it helps, you and Gunther have been more than we could have hoped for," Devana said. "I am grateful that the survival of our world rests in your hands."

# CHAPTER 4

"I DON'T UNDERSTAND HOW SOMETHING AS important as the future of the paranormal and human worlds is always couched in such ridiculous mystical gobbledygook," I told Aidan. The two of us drove toward Tabitha's parents' house. Gunther and Kyle went to the police precinct to find out any additional information (and scout the locked cell phone) while Aidan and I visited Tabitha's parents.

"It's the nature of mysteries," Aidan said as we drove along Main Street. "Mysticism itself *means* to conceal. Well, the Greek word it came from, anyway."

"I don't need an etymology lesson, Aidan."

"I'm not trying to give you one. All I'm saying is that hidden truths have a long and illustrious history. I mean, technically, *you* are a mystery. So am I. The entire circus is a mystery."

"Not really," I disagreed. "The humans can walk onto the fairgrounds and ride a ride and pet a were-elephant. They can even eat magical food."

"They don't *know* they're petting a were-elephant. Or eating magical food."

"But they can *see* both. If it's right in front of you, *how* is it a mystery?"

"You didn't take many philosophy courses in college did you?" Aidan laughed.

"I avoided the philosophy department like the plague," I told him. I watched the old country storefronts slowly pass by the window. This was only the second time I was back in the *real world* since becoming a ringmaster. The first time was when Aidan and Kyle joined the circus. We even picked up Cama the death bat when the trip ended.

I wondered what this trip would change.

I felt bad for a moment thinking of the Texas streets and storefronts as the real world. It was a phrase that always upset Anya every time I mistakenly uttered it. Yet when you contrasted millions of humans to just thousands of paranormals, a hundred and ninety-two countries compared to just a few paranormal villages and towns…this would *always* be the real world to me.

Even if I didn't live in it anymore.

"Are you one of those 'philosophy is irrelevant' people?" Aidan turned right on Hightower Street.

"No, I'm one of those 'give me a test with multiple choice answers' people." I pointed toward the large gray house at the end of the road. "That's where her parents live. She invited me to a party there once."

Aidan nodded and slowly pulled in to the large driveway and parked the car. "Do you have any idea what you will say to them?"

I stared out the car window at the big house from my past. I didn't know what Tabitha may have told her parents about our friendship, or its demise. Since she and I were older when we met, I didn't know her parents well. I would recognize them well enough if we came across each other in a store, but that was the extent.

Tabitha hadn't talked about them much. I knew Darius Stevens was a distant father, a programmer at an Austin tech company. My friend used to complain that she would have got more attention from her father if she had been lines of code as opposed to a person. Tabitha's mother, Sarah, however…I knew they were close. Depending on what Tabitha told her, she might not be happy to see me.

"I don't know what I'm going to say," I sighed and reached for the door. "I just hope they let us help."

~

The large white double front doors opened as Aidan and I made our way up the sidewalk. The tear-stained face of Sarah Stevens stared back at me from within the hallway. "Charlotte? Charlotte! Is that you? Oh, I'm so glad to see you alive!"

Well. That wasn't the reaction I was expecting. Tabitha's mother was ecstatic to see me. I could feel her excitement wash over me, an excitement at odds with her tear-stained face and sad outward demeanor.

"Mrs. Stevens, someone got word to me about Tabitha's disappearance and I came home as soon as I heard," I told her when we reached the front porch. "Well, Aidan and I both. I'm not sure if you ever met him."

"The gay fake boyfriend? I heard about him, but no, we've never met." Mrs. Stevens looked Aidan up and down through wet eyes. "Please, both of you, come in. I'm so sorry for the state of the house." Tabitha's mother waved toward the immaculate, shining hallway where every painting and single bit of bric-à-brac appeared to have a permanent place. "I just haven't been able to bring myself to do any cleaning the past few days."

If this was a bad state, I wondered what the place looked like when it met Sarah Stevens' definition of clean.

As she led us into the front parlor, our feet made footprints in the rigid lines of the vacuumed cream-colored carpeting. There wasn't so much as a speck of dust anywhere, and the traditional furniture surrounding the mirror-polished wood coffee table appeared as if no rear end had ever dented it. The room was picture-perfect, decorated and cleaned to optimum display. It wouldn't have looked out of place as a set in a furniture store.

It felt...sterile.

"Please, have a seat." Mrs. Stevens gestured to the loveseat. As Mrs. Stevens' breath hit me, the strong scent of alcohol invaded my nose. The emotional woman sat down unsteadily on a chair to the right of us. "I wishhh you had got the message from Tabitha before she disappeared, but you'll be able to stay until she comes home. I am sure she'll be home any day now. Yes, yes, any day." Sarah Stevens rubbed a small adhesive patch on her forearm as she murmured her surety that Tabitha would come home.

"A message?" I asked, confused.

Mrs. Stevens stared at me in shock, her pupils dilated. "Why, of courssse. Tabitha has been trying to get a hold of you since you disappeared on Halloween of last year," the woman said while only slightly slurring her words. "I know you upset her at first, Charlotte, but surrrely you didn't think she would stay angry."

"I did," I told her and glanced at Aidan in confusion. "She told me that she never wanted to talk to me again. I mean…if that changed, if she wanted to talk to me, Tabitha could have sent a message through my parents."

"Your parents," Mrs. Stevens whispered, her eyes darting around. "Tabitha was afraid that your parents had…had…well, had done something *terrible* to you. She went to speak to them a few days after Halloween but there was no one in the house. When she went around back, she saw your father…" Mrs. Stevens' eyes cast around the room as if someone would overhear.

"She saw my father what?" I asked her. Aidan shifted next to me, and I could feel his energy turn defensive.

"Your f-f-father was controlling the beastsss," she whispered, her face white and her words slurring even more. Shuddering, Mrs. Stevens reached to the side table and grabbed a glass filled with a brown liquid and ice.

Fear gripped me as Tabitha's mother implied my friend had seen my father using magic. What's more, she had told someone about what she saw. Tabitha told her mother. How many more people had Tabitha told?

"Is Mr. Stevens at home?" I asked the drunk woman.

"Darius?" she asked and then threw back the rest of her drink. Slamming the glass down on the pristine sofa table, her eyes blazed with anger and her hand returned to the small transdermal patch on her arm. "Nothing stops Darius from work. Not even the disappearance of his own daughter."

Aidan kicked me under the coffee table, and I reached out to sample Mrs. Stevens energy, thoughts and emotions. It was something I had wanted to avoid as I suspected Tabitha's mother's pain, even just a portion, would be unpleasant to experience. Now, everything about this situation seemed...wrong. Using magic to pry was necessary.

We needed to know more about what had been going on with Tabitha in the past year, and her drunk mother was all we had to work with at the moment.

"What do you mean, my father was controlling beasts?" I asked Mrs. Stevens, hoping she was so drunk she wouldn't remember this conversation.

"The animals, he would speak, and they would respond as if they were *human*," she answered, her hands squeezing into fists. "But dogs, they can't do that, can they?" In her mind, she pictured a hundred dogs in front of my father, sitting and staring at him like an obedient army. "The dogs in your shelter, something possessed them! Tabitha knew something terrible had happened to you, something awful! Until she knew whether your parents were responsible, how could she have trusted them?"

I drew in a long breath and exhaled, trying to calm myself. Tabitha was never a religious or spiritual person, but if she caught Dad training the dogs using his witch power...well, it would freak anybody out. Especially if that person didn't think something like that was possible. Dad was always careful to do it in the indoor play shelter, an area that was not accessible to the public.

But Tabitha knew me and had been over to visit often. She was at ease on the shelter grounds. She would've felt comfortable going to look for my parents, and she would not have stopped for a sign that said no one could go any further.

"What did she do when she saw this...thing she thinks she saw?" I asked Mrs. Stevens.

"She was determined to save you," Mrs. Stevens said, bobbing her head as she pointed at me. "She went to the church, but they laughed at us. Told her she should get counseling, or see a psychiatrist because she must be crazy. Tabitha, *my* daughter! Crazy! As if there is nothing left in life that is unexplainable! As if demons don't exist in the world!" she hissed, glancing toward the entryway.

"Mrs. Stevens, she may have seen something she misinterpreted as unexplainable, but—"

"Where have you been, Charlotte Astley?" she spat. She wrapped her arms around herself. The woman's hands were shaking, and she swayed in the chair, her dilated eyes narrowing. "And *you*, fake boyfriend? You disappeared, as well! And you, Charlotte, you showed up for just a few days and someone killed Tiffany Drake! Then someone killed Anthony Drake! Someone saw you with that *horrible* Michael Hayden, and then you disappeared again!"

"I..."

I was at a loss.

Any explanations I could give for what Mrs. Stevens was saying were answers I wasn't allowed to give to a human. I could see how our previous visit looked from the outside, especially since the homicides of Tiffany and Anthony Drake were likely not reported on well because of who they were. "There're explanations for everything, Mrs. Stevens, and I can assure you there's nothing that suspicious about—"

"There is an evil here in Mickwac," Mrs. Stevens said, cutting me off. Her chest rose and fell with rapid breaths as she stared at me. "Tabitha was determined to understand the evil here, to banish it, to find you and Aidan and break you from the grips of..."

Sarah trailed off and stared into the distance.

"What do you mean? How did she mean to do that, Mrs. Stevens?"

"The witches were the *only ones that would believe her,*" Mrs. Stevens whispered. She raked her fingers through her hair. My blood ran cold when the word witch left the drunk woman's lips. "She didn't have a choice. She worked with the witches at Avalon Grove. She worked with them and worked with them and worked with them to understand what was happening here—"

"And then she disappeared," Darius Stevens said from the hallway. "No thanks to you, Sarah."

Sarah Stevens pressed a hand to her throat as if to strangle a sob already dancing across the lines of her face. "Don't say that, you can't say that, Darius," she whispered, rocking back and forth on the fancy chair. "It wasn't my crime, it wasn't! How can you say that to me, Darius, how can you say—"

"Have another drink, Sarah," Tabitha's father said. He tugged his tie loose. "That and entertaining our daughter's ridiculous imagination seem to be the only two things you're good at."

I felt Darius's insult stab into her like a knife. A chaos of anger, pain, fear and obsessive love exploded within the inebriated woman who stared at her husband and wept.

"Mr. Stevens, perhaps we should go," I said and stood up. We could have discovered more information from Tabitha's parents that would be useful, but at the moment I was feeling like I knew more than I wanted about Tabitha's home life, and this couple's marriage. Aidan rose next to me and we walked toward the man standing in the way of our exit.

"It appears neither of you have been sucked into some paranormal portal or captured by a demon, I see." Darius Stevens looked Aidan and me over. "When Tabitha is found, I hope that she'll realize all this study and talk of witches and magic has all been a gigantic waste of time. *If* she's found, in any case."

"What you mean, *if* she's found?" I shot back. My shoulders tensed and I drilled my telepathic power into the cold man. Tabitha had told me that her father was distant and somewhat disinterested in her, but I was gobsmacked at the sociopathic level of apathy I was sensing from Darius Stevens about the safety and return of his daughter. "Do you not care whether your daughter is dead or alive?"

"Tabitha is an adult," Darius Stevens responded. He strode over to the wet bar I hadn't spotted before and poured himself a drink. His emotions were calm, and his attitude toward me cocky. "Her decisions are her own, and if the girl is dead, I know it was her own stupid choices to join a cult and believe in fairy tales that put her in the ground. At least she will no longer be the mistake she was to this family, dashing around with hippies and dancing in the moonlight."

As Darius Stevens raised his shoulder in a half shrug, I fought an intense desire to clobber the man.

Tabitha? Tabitha Stevens an embarrassment as a daughter? The Tabitha I knew was honorable, smart, accomplished. She had graduated from college summa cum laude. She not only volunteered at our animal shelter, she volunteered to serve Thanksgiving and Christmas dinners to the homeless in Austin...

Though after meeting her parents, I could see there may have been more than just one reason for Tabitha's choice to skip family holidays in favor of humanitarianism.

I was so astounded by Darius Stevens I couldn't even find an appropriate way to respond. I stared at the man, my jaw slightly dropped, unsure of what to say. I felt with certainty that no words I could come up with would make a dent in this man's coldness.

"Come on, Charlotte, let's go," Aidan whispered and lightly gripped my elbow. "I think nothing else that we find out here will help us."

"Help you what?" Darius asked, sipping his bourbon. His eyes narrowed as he waited for my answer.

"*Find your daughter,*" I said tightly and tears filled my eyes. I had been so concerned about respecting Tabitha's boundaries, respecting her privacy, and hiding my own powers that I had rarely ever rummaged around in her emotions or her mind. She hid the pain of these two horrible people as parents well. I never would've guessed these two human beings, one a sociopath and one a drunk, had raised the incredible person I knew,.

"It's no wonder you and Tabitha were friends." Darius held up his glass as if to make a toast. "Your arrogance must have bound you together."

"If Tabitha was arrogant, it looks like she came by it honestly," I snapped. My eyes flashed with anger. Aidan's grip on my elbow grew tighter, and he propelled me toward the front door.

"Touché, Ms. Astley," Darius called from behind me. I mumbled several four-letter words under my breath while Aidan opened the door so we could escape.

"Come back anytime!" Sarah called from the parlor.

# CHAPTER 5

"WHAT WAS *THAT*?" I ASKED. AIDAN BACKED US OUT of the large gray house's driveway. "Did Tabitha ever mention to you that her parents were…"

"Crazy? Horrible? Psychotic?" Aidan offered. He glanced back over his shoulder and backed the car into the street a little quicker than he needed to. "If you asked me two hours ago what Tabitha's parents were like, even with my powers…I mean, I never would've guessed anything close to the two human beings we met. You said you'd been here before and met them, though."

"I came to a Christmas party one winter, and met them briefly," I told Aidan, gazing back to the house once more. I could make out a dark figure, tall, staring out from behind the sheer curtains draped in front of the bay window of the parlor. I was almost sure the person gazing out at our escape was Darius Stevens, but the man's energy was so unpleasant I didn't want to confirm. "They were pleasant enough, I guess. I mean, they were entertaining, like, a hundred people. People hosting a party act like people hosting a party, I guess."

"Didn't you reach out to examine their energy or anything?"

"That wasn't something I did when I lived in the human world," I told Aidan. The further we traveled from the Stevens' house, the better I felt. It was as if the home had an oppressive, dark energy that had lived there long before Tabitha had disappeared. "I used it a lot with the animals at the animal shelter—"

"You seemed to have no problem using it on me when we went out," Aidan said, droving back through Main Street. His tone was matter of fact, but I sensed a little annoyance.

"I have to reach out to people if I want to know something, but sometimes someone's thought is so strong that it's broadcast almost like a radio blaring." We drove through the town square. "You thinking the bartender was cute? You *advertised* that."

"Okay, I'll give you that one," Aidan chuckled. "He was cute."

"Talking of how powers work—wait, what's that? That spooky-looking store over there?" I pointed to a storefront in the old town center. A bronze statue of a goddess stood next to the dark wood door of the red brick storefront. Bay windows with shutters painted black gave the place a sinister look. Thick green vines crept along the front wall, and a large pillar candle flickered from the center of the window.

"It looks like one of those Wiccan shops," Aidan said.

"Yeah, but look at the name."

A wooden sign with carved Celtic-flavored lettering announced the name of the store.

And the name of the store was Avalon Grove.

"We were so shocked at Tabitha having crazy parents, we didn't talk about what Tabitha's mother said," I told Aidan. He pulled into a parking spot in front of the magic shop. "She saw my dad talking to the animals, and Mrs. Stevens thinks Tabitha thought my parents were evil. Like, supernatural evil."

"Considering who Tabitha's parents are, it's easy to understand why she would think that," Aidan said. He turned the car off and set the emergency brake, but he didn't move to get out. "You don't think she poked around into what happened to us too deeply and the Witches' Council did something to her, do you?"

I stared at the pillar candle glow and thought I saw it flash. Aidan's question was more paranoia than a serious theory about what happened to Tabitha, but his question made me uncomfortable all the same. I didn't answer.

"Look, all we know right now is that she's been gone for two days, her parents are nuts, and one of her nutty parents said she looked into human occult studies. We know nothing about her life, though, beyond that. We haven't seen her in over a year."

"So what do you propose?" Aidan asked.

"Well, that's the area occult shop," I pointed to the spooky storefront. "I suggest we go in there and ask if they know her."

"Just like that?"

"Just like that."

Aidan pulled the keys out of the ignition and reached for the door.

～

The tinkling of bells reverberated through the narrow store as we pushed the creaking door open. The thick perfume of frankincense and myrrh hit me before my foot was even through the threshold.

"Welcome to Avalon Grove," a deep voice called from the back of the store. The floor was an old wood one, and it was dingy, as if no one had bothered to wax it for years. Our footsteps echoed as we walked further in to the chamber of incense and crystals and cauldrons. There were no other visitors. "Is there anything I can help you with?"

I sighted the man speaking and did my best not to react to the air of fake royalty he wrapped around himself like a cloak. The gothically-dressed raven-haired proprietor sat in a red velvet Baroque chair that looked more like a throne, high-backed with glittering gold wood trim. There was a small table in front of him, and a smaller Victorian-style chair with red velvet across from him.

It, however, lacked the high back and gold trim of his own chosen post.

"I hope so," I told him. I picked my way through the display tables. "I have a friend who's gone missing, and someone told me she had been spending time here. Her name is Tabitha Stevens."

The man raised one pierced eyebrow, but didn't respond.

"Do you know her?" A long pause followed my question as the man studied me.

I waited.

"If I did, I wouldn't be able to tell you," the man said. He leaned forward and pushed himself up, his all-black outfit peeling away from the red velvet chair in a slow, liquid movement. "I am oath-bound to all those who come into this hallowed space. I hold their privacy as I would my own."

"This is a store," I said with some irritation. "I'm not asking for her credit card number, just if you know her.

"As I've already told you, that is a question I cannot answer," the man said. "Do you have other questions, or can I help you with something? A spell to find something lost, perhaps?"

I rolled my eyes.

"Sir, perhaps we started off on the wrong foot," Aidan said as he stepped forward and extended his hand to the pale twenty-something. "My name is Aidan Parker. And you are?"

The man's face went white, even whiter than

it already was—and it astonished me that a more colorless shade was even possible.

"You are Aidan Parker? But...but...you are missing! You've been missing for months! Our coven was sure that Michael Hayden or the people that took Charlotte killed you!" The shop owner put his hand out against the counter to steady himself while he gawked at Aidan.

So much for this guy's privacy respectfulness.

"What does that mean? So you know Tabitha?" I asked him. He glanced at me.

"She's with me, friend," Aidan told the man without pointing out that I was the Charlotte he believed taken. I leaned over the case and Aidan placed a possessive hand on my arm. "Please, give me the honor of your name."

"Raven," the man told him. "My name is Raven Goodfellow."

"Of course it is," I rolled my eyes. Aidan shot me a look of annoyance as his foot careened into my own. I understood that he was trying to build a rapport with the pasty-faced goth, but I remembered people like this from college.

I avoided them.

Aidan was right, though, and his kick was a reminder for me to turn on my telepathic BS detector. This idiot knew Tabitha, and we needed to get whatever information he might have. I forced a smile on my face, sighed, and I stretched my power into his emo mind.

"Raven, it is a pleasure to meet you," Aidan said. The men shook again. "Allow me to introduce my friend, Charlotte Astley. She's not missing, either."

"Yeah, how you doing?" I nodded without extending my hand.

"It can't be!" Shock, hope, fear slithered through him. His eyes enlarged, his pupils dilated, and his breathing quickened. His lithe figure vibrated as he stared down at me. He stepped back, then forward, then back, then forward, as if his brain couldn't process whether he wanted to move closer or run away. "You can't be Charlotte Astley. You can't be!"

"Well, I am," I confessed.

"You are the daughter of the soul speaker!" Awe poured from the goth.

"I'm the daughter of the what now?"

"Your father can speak to the souls of the animals, their spirits. You must be the successor to a great magic! Are you fae? Are you even human at all?" Raven stepped forward, his hands shaking as he committed to a course of action.

His fingers trembled, he reached toward my arm, and I felt obsessive threat pouring from him.

"Dude, don't touch me," I warned him, leaning back.

"Please," he whispered, his eyes smoldering with demand. "I have to know if you are human."

"Hey," I raised my voice and stepped back. "I'm not joking around. Don't touch me."

"Do you sacrifice the animals?" Raven whispered, his eyes careening around the store as if someone could walk in and overhear. His emotions veered within him, bubbling up in explosive waves. "The ones at the shelter, do they walk into the fire? Throw themselves on the knife for the gods?"

Nauseated at Raven's suggestion, I wrenched my talent out of this nasty little pretend-witch. "Dude, what is wrong with you? We run an animal shelter! A no-kill animal shelter—we don't sacrifice animals. That's revolting!"

"You must, you have to...how else would your father gain the power he has?" Raven's eyes darted between me and Aidan. Raven gasped. "Are you *truly* not mortal? Is that the reason? You must reveal it to me!"

The pasty-faced idiot reached for me again,

just as the front door squeaked and the bells clanged.

"Raven, leave them alone," a short, round woman barked before the door had even closed. She strode with heavy, echoing steps toward us, her eyes boring into Raven.

"Samantha, I—"

"I need not be psychic to know what you were doing, Raven," the woman said. As she joined us, I noticed the resemblance between the forty-something woman and the twenty-something Raven. Though he was tall, pale, with blue-black dyed hair and she was round, short, and blonde, they were clearly related. Their facial features were near mirror images of one another. "You should be grateful that Tabitha's mother called me to let me know Charlotte and Aidan were looking for Tabitha. That way I could get here before you did something stupid."

"Mrs. Stevens called you?" I asked her. She nodded.

"Mom, please, let me—"

"Raven, go upstairs to the residence and let me talk to Aidan and Charlotte," Samantha told her son. His brows drew together and his eyes blazed with anger. "Don't. Just do as I say."

"I'm not a *child*, Mother."

"You're not a high priest of this coven, either, and this is coven business," Samantha told him, gathering herself up to her full height...short though that was. "I am the high priestess, and you'll show me the proper respect by doing what I say. Go to the apartment, get lunch. We'll talk about this later."

Raven clenched his fists as he stared his mother down. Then as a single second passed on a nearby clock, his hands relaxed and he shrugged. It was as if the storm of emotions had stilled within him in the blink of an eye. With a smile at his mother and a nod to Aidan and me, he sauntered toward the front door and left Avalon Grove without another word.

"My apologies for anything that happened before I got here," Samantha Goodfellow told us. She waved us toward the table. "My son means well, but since he got out of rehab life's been difficult for him. Sarah assumed that you would head here once you left her house, and I wanted to make sure I was here."

It surprised me Tabitha's mother was sober enough to make a phone call, much less recount what we discussed. Or that she made any guesses as to our next stop. *Why didn't she just suggest that we come here and talk to these folks if she was so sure we'd show up here?* I wondered.

"You know Sarah Stevens?" I asked her as we moved toward the table. Samantha gestured for me to take the throne-chair. Aidan settled into the other velvet chair, and Samantha pulled out a folding chair from behind a bookcase.

"I do, poor woman," she answered once we were seated. "As I suspect you guessed by now, I also know Tabitha."

"Do you know where she is?" Aidan asked.

"If I did, I would've called the police," she told Aidan. She drew in a long breath and then exhaled. "I suppose you to want to know what she's been doing for the last year."

"If you can tell us," I said.

"I can tell you," Samantha answered, and then paused. She glanced at the front window as two women looked in, interested in the wares of the shop or the three of us speaking. I couldn't tell which.

The chubby high priestess frowned.

Getting up again, she shuffled to the front door and locked it, flipping a glitter-decorated sign hanging from a peg to "Closed." Walking back toward us, she gestured toward the door behind Raven's throne-chair. "Let's head into the storeroom instead. I'd prefer the passersby not see the three of us speaking."

"I've known Darius and Sarah since college," Samantha began. We settled into camping chairs strewn around the magical storeroom. "They are members of this coven. Technically, anyhow."

"Darius Stevens is a Wiccan?" I didn't intend the question to sound as skeptical as it did, but I'd known Wiccans in college. They were pleasant, environmentally aware, and hippie-like in their attitude to life.

Darius Stevens didn't have a gentle hippie-like bone in his body.

"He never formally left, so, yes," Samantha said and then gazed at one of the largest amethyst rocks I had ever seen. "At first I thought he only joined because of his attraction to Sarah. They were both members of the coven before they married, you see."

"But you don't think so now?"

"I think Darius Stevens joined the coven because he believed he would gain power," Samantha said and shuddered. "Once he realized we were just a bunch of feminist women that gathered together to celebrate the divine feminine and to help one another, he was no longer interested."

"But Sarah was," Aidan said. His expression hardened.

"Yes, she was," Samantha nodded, her face flushed. "Our coven wasn't something she joined to pass the time in college, like so many. Sarah found solace and joy in the goddess's worship. She found comfort in the friendship of her sisters. Darius grew jealous at first, and then..." Samantha's voice trailed off.

"He struck me as a judgmental and condescending kind of guy," I told her and the anger rolled through me again. "He came in while we were talking to Sarah, and the way he treated her was just awful."

"Sarah sneaks away for a full moon or Sabbat now and again, usually when Darius is off on a business trip trying to become master of the world," Samantha rolled her eyes. "We do what we can to help her, but what solace she used to find in the goddess and in her sisters she now finds mostly at the bottom of a bottle, poor woman. Addiction is a terrible thing."

"When did they leave? Or at least stop coming together?"

"When Darius Stevens realized being known as a kookie hippie would negatively impact his climb up the corporate ladder. I think Tabitha was seven or eight, perhaps? Maybe as old as ten years old. She was a young thing," Samantha sighed.

"Old enough to remember her parents being pagan," I said to Aidan.

"Old enough to remember her father denigrating it," he answered.

"Yes, Tabitha remembered all. She remembered the circles we used to have, and the other children, and the celebrations. She lost most of her close friends when her father decided they could no longer attend," Samantha said, anger coiling like a snake through her words. "Tabitha and Sarah would pray in secret far from Darius's eyes, at least at first. Eventually, Tabitha found new friends and Sarah found new ways to cope."

"I knew none of this. Did you?" I looked at Aidan. He shook his head no.

"Tabitha was always a good girl. She learned about privacy early in the coven. After all, we are pagans in a state that doesn't exactly welcome those who are different. Our faith is not something we need to wave a flag about," she smiled. "I imagine the practice of keeping private that which others didn't need to know was something that was second nature to her."

"Forgive me for saying so, but you're not exactly private with your beliefs." I gestured around the storeroom at the incense, ritual items, pagan statues and candles stored there. "The whole town knows where this place is and that you own it."

"Someone has to be open," Samantha told me, her smile tired. "Since no one else was doing it, I decided it might as well be me. Most people live their life without magic or mystery in it, and they do just fine. Some people, though, need more. By having the shop I make it a little easier for those people to find it. Like your friend Tabitha."

"Has Tabitha been coming here all along?"

"No," Samantha shook her head. "She only came here in the last year. Well, she was here when she was a small child, like I told you. As an adult, as a seeker? Just last year. It was Tabitha's concern about you initially, and then when Aidan also disappeared with no notice it concerned her further."

"Why would it?" Aidan asked.

Samantha leaned forward on her camping chair and placed her chin on her hands. Sadness clouded her features as she looked back and forth between us, searching our eyes for something I couldn't sense. Finally, the corner of her mouth turned up.

"She knew what your father was," Samantha told me. "I know that you cannot acknowledge what your father is, or your mother, or…or what *you* are. But she saw, and she knew enough about magic to know what she saw."

Aidan and I looked at each other, our expressions mirroring false ease as our eyes glinted with concern. I didn't know how much this human woman knew about the paranormal world, the Witches' Council, and what we were. I also didn't care about breaking the rules regarding myself, not really, and I probably would have just admitted it to her if I could.

It wasn't about what I wanted.

The Witches' Council would kill humans that knew the truth about us. I couldn't admit to this woman what we were. It wasn't safe for her, or my family in the human world.

What freaked me out, though, was that she didn't even *ask* if we were what she thought we were. If Samantha Goodfellow was that sure of what we were, *so sure* she didn't even bother to ask a question…did that mean Tabitha was as well?

And if Tabitha talked to the wrong person about this…

Resentment pounded within me like a drumbeat. No matter where I went, no matter what happened, no matter how far away I got from Imperatorial City and the Witches' Council, the threat of Mina World and her cruel laws and punishments followed me.

# CHAPTER 6

"I can't believe I didn't know Tabitha was a Wiccan," Aidan said when we pulled away from the Avalon Grove store. Samantha Goodfellow's pale face stared at us from the wind-chime-lined window, her eyes locked with mine. Her expression was closed, but the hint of a scowl remained.

"There's a lot of stuff we're finding out today that I'm having trouble believing," I answered. "I don't understand why my parents didn't just call me on the cauldron and let me know Tabitha was looking for me. I feel like all of this could've been avoided if they had. She never would have gone into the shelter, and never would have seen—"

"Don't blame your parents, Charlotte."

"I will blame *myself* if Mina has got a hold of Tabitha." We pulled onto the main road. "Though how the Witches' Council justifies killing human beings just because they know we exist is beyond me. I mean, you heard Samantha. They base their entire religion on the fact that they think we exist."

"They have *faith* we exist," Aidan said. "That's different from knowing."

"Is it, though?"

Aidan didn't respond to my question, but that didn't surprise me. I didn't understand how his power worked or to what extent he had access to the truth of the universe, but I suspected it was more than I knew and less than he was comfortable with.

"It's getting late, and we haven't had lunch yet." Aidan pointed toward a hamburger stand to our right. "I know I haven't had one of Moocow's burgers in a long time. Want to stop?"

"Sure. Hey, you know, you can get anything you want from Jeannie, even one of those burgers."

"I don't like magic food," Aidan said, pulling into the hamburger joint's parking lot. "It seems like it's missing something. Even when it's not."

They located Moocow's, a staple hamburger

joint of this small town, right next to Anthony Drake's Italian restaurant. Drake's "business" looked much different from the way it was the last time I was here, and I wasn't here all that long ago. It was cleaner, painted a much lighter and brighter color than before. The Mafia-owned restaurant appeared as popular as ever. The parking lot was full and locals nodded to one another as they entered and left.

"My bet is Michael Hayden took it over like he took over everything," Aidan said when he caught me looking. The place had been the scene of an uncomfortable confrontation with Anthony Drake, the previous criminal Godfather of this small strip of Texas. "He didn't strike me as a guy that would leave anything on the table."

"No, I guess not," I shrugged and looked away.

We ordered our burgers at the counter and slid into one of the old, beat-up booths toward the back with our vanilla colas. As I glanced out the window at the sights and sounds I once knew, it surprised me to realize that it didn't feel like home anymore.

Familiar, yes. Comfortingly nostalgic.

But not home.

Maybe Anya was right. Maybe this wasn't my real world.

"Penny for your thoughts?" Aidan's question poked into my memories. I looked back at my friend. His brows drew together in a look of concern.

"I don't know, I didn't expect Tabitha's life to have changed so much," I told Aidan, keeping hidden my uncomfortable distance from all I had known before the Magical Midway. "And for someone who hated being lied to, it sure seems like she was keeping an awful lot from us."

"It seems there was a lot about Tabitha that we didn't know," Aidan agreed. He took in a deep breath and exhaled. "Maybe the reason we upset her so much by hiding our true relationship was because it reminded her of what *she* was hiding."

"I don't believe that," I crossed my arms over my chest. "You can't believe that's why she was upset. We lied to her. She hates liars. She had every right to be upset about that."

"Well, I don't know—Bobby was the one that read me the riot act. Tabitha never spoke to me at all after the truth came out, so I'm just taking a guess here based on what we're finding out today." Aidan turned his head and cast his own gaze upon the world we didn't live in anymore. "People hide a lot of things, Charlotte. And they don't like to be reminded they're doing it."

A uninterested high school girl plunked two baskets of greasy burgers and fries down on the table between us. She snatched the number off her table without so much as a glance in our direction and then walked away.

"People live in their own world," Aidan gestured to the distracted blonde teenager. "And in everyone's world, they are the center of it."

"After everything Samantha Goodfellow just told us, you think Tabitha was completely wrapped up in herself?"

"Not completely," he said as he wrapped his hands around the hamburger in front of him. "Look, people aren't completely narcissistic *all* the time. But if you're looking for an explanation for their behavior because you don't understand why they did what they did, most of the time it lies within their own past, their *own* issues. That's all I'm saying."

"Okay, so, going with your premise, then. Why did Tabitha think what my father did was evil? Why did her mind automatically go to demons or possession or whatever she was afraid of? She *knew* my dad, Aidan. My mom, my dad. She'd been over dozens of times. Suddenly she's afraid of him?"

"So, going with my premise, the answer is

simple." Aidan wiped smears of mustard from his mouth. Throwing down the napkin, he cocked his head and stared into my eyes.

"Well?" I asked him impatiently.

"Tabitha has seen evil. She's seen real magic, and the person that wielded it was evil."

"And so she was afraid."

"Exactly."

I jumped at a loud knock on the window to find Kyle grinning and waving a piece of paper.

"I thought I might find you here," Kyle said. He and Gunther slid in to the booth with us. "You're predictable, Aidan Parker."

Aidan blushed and smiled at the centaur.

*He had a little help,* Gunther thought with a wink. *I peeked and described where the two of you were.*

*Let's keep that our little secret,* I thought back. I watched Aidan and Kyle lean into each other like an old married couple. *I wouldn't want to spoil how impressed Aidan is.*

"You two are talking in your heads, aren't you?" Kyle turned to us. "That drives me nuts. I can, like, *feel* the conversation is going on but I can't *hear* anything."

"Dude, keep your voice down!" I looked around the half-full restaurant to see if Kyle's statement had registered with anyone. After a few seconds, I sighed with relief and motioned to Kyle to keep his voice down. "Overactive detective Spidey sense?" I raised my eyebrow.

Kyle laughed. "Maybe something like that."

"How did it go with Tabitha's parents?"

"Oh, man, *that* was something else." Aidan tilted his head and exhaled sharply. "There are *definitely* some issues at the Stevens household."

"You met Darius Stevens, I take it?" Kyle asked.

"You know him? Why didn't you say anything?"

"I don't know him personally or anything like that." Kyle grabbed Aidan's vanilla Coke and took a long slurp. Shaking the cup at the end, he sighed and grabbed all of our cups. "I heard about him. He's been involved in some lawsuits, and some guys on the force have had to assist with subpoenas. Guy has a reputation as quite a jerk."

Kyle took our cups back up to the counter for refills.

"Hey, Aidan," I whispered across the table.

"Yeah?"

"I like him," I smiled warmly at my friend. He ducked so I wouldn't see the blush that had returned to his face. "I don't think I'd told you that straight out."

"No, I guess, not really. You hadn't."

"I like him, too, not that anyone really cares all that much about my opinion," Gunther said seriously, tugging at his shirt collar. I elbowed him, and he held up his hands in defeat, laughing. "He's a smart guy, and he got us into the evidence room raising no alarms at all. The humans take that evidence room seriously."

"They do," Kyle said as he brought back the full sodas and sat down next to Aidan. "I'm well-liked, though. And look at this mug." He jutted his chin out. "I have a *very* trustworthy face, I'll have you know."

"That must come in handy when you're trying to do something illegal," I said sarcastically.

"Totally," he nodded. "It totally, absolutely does. Remember, I was the Pollyanna on the force against all the corruption. None of those guys in a million years would believe I broke into an evidence locker. No way."

Kyle Roberts was not the buttoned up, dour, sour detective I had reconnected with during the

Tiffany Drake murder inquest. He wasn't even the obnoxious, cocky football player I had known in high school. Meeting Aidan, realizing he was a centaur, joining the Magical Midway…it all seemed to have anchored him into a comfort with who and what he was.

*We are all just looking for a place we belong,* Gunther thought. He reached below the table and squeezed my hand.

*That doesn't bode well for you and me,* I thought back. *We belong in different places.*

Gunther didn't respond.

"Hey, what's with the sad faces? Yes, okay, Tabitha is still missing. That was probably a stupid thing for me to say," Kyle said as he pulled a folded piece of paper out of his pocket. "But your boyfriend, here, magically pulled Tabitha's phone calls in and out from her phone and shoved them on this piece of paper. It was impressive."

"What did you find?" Aidan asked.

"The last couple of days before she went missing it looks like Tabitha only spoke to a few different people. Well, four numbers," Kyle corrected. Pointing to the paper, he continued. "Her mom, her dad, her dad's office, and a store. Actually, the store's kind of weird—"

"Avalon Grove," I guessed.

Kyle looked up sharply. "Yeah, how did you know?"

"We just came from there, actually," Aidan told him.

"Tabitha was investigating what happened to me and Aidan."

"What do you mean, what happened to you and Aidan?" Gunther asked.

"She called my house looking for me a year ago, right after I became ringmaster," I said, lowering my voice. "I guess she thought my parents' answers about where I was and why I couldn't be contacted were sketchy, so she came over to the animal shelter to talk to them."

"She saw Charlotte's dad doing…you know, stuff." Aidan leaned toward Kyle.

"Stuff? Like what stuff?"

"You know," my eyes widened, and I flapped my hands around. "Stuff." Gunther chuckled next to me and I elbowed him again. "You have a better way to explain it without explaining it? Go right ahead."

"Oh, right," Kyle nodded thoughtfully. "*Stuff.* Well, that's not good."

"There is more, actually," I told him.

"Quite a bit," Aidan agreed.

"Maybe we should head back to your parents' place so we can talk without risk of others overhearing." Kyle pushed himself out of the booth and stood up. "Charlotte needs to…um… see the sun go down. We can go over what we know until then."

"I think we should take a drive out to where they found Tabitha's car tonight," I told them as Gunther helped me out of the booth. "I want to see what it looks like at night. Maybe I'll be able to spot something that the police couldn't."

"That's a good idea," Kyle nodded.

As I slipped behind the wheel of my mother's car, Gunther cocked his head.

"What?" I asked him. The engine of the old Toyota sputtered to life. Kyle and Aidan pulled out in my father's shelter truck, and I backed the car up without hitting anything even though I hadn't driven in over a year. I considered that an accomplishment.

"Nothing," he said. As we pulled out into the street, he slapped his hands down on his thighs so loudly that I jumped. "That's not true. How are you able to keep from despair while your friend is missing? Possibly hurt? Maybe even dead?"

Gunther's eyes scanned the humans walking on either side of the road, and I appreciated the intensity with which he searched for Tabitha. The problem was that I felt he was searching intently so he had an excuse to avert his eyes from me. "Freaking out won't help the situation," I said distractedly.

"No, I agree, but sometimes…I don't know, Charlotte, sometimes I'm in awe of how you approach things. You don't seem to let anything get to you." Pain flashed in him but before I could get a hold to read why, it was gone. I wondered if I had sensed it in the first place.

"You don't, either," I said. We merged onto the highway toward my parents' house. "You're one of the calmest people I've ever known, Gunther." *Which is crazy considering what you've been through,* I thought to myself. My boyfriend had seen his mother killed right in front of him as a child by Mina World. Though he didn't know what Mina World had done…

I pushed the thought out in case Gunther was listening to the musings in my head. He didn't know, and I didn't want him to know yet. We had enough to deal with, and it was up to Gerda to tell him if she wanted him to know.

"I may be calm, but that doesn't mean I'm not falling victim to despair at times," he said hesitantly, his normally clear voice sounding… strange.

"Despair is a strong word, Gunther. Are you okay?" I reached out with my nosy telepathic tendrils and touched a deep well of sadness that flashed within Gunther like the lightning bolts of a Texas summer storm. Just like the transitory Texas weather, the sadness I had felt was gone just as quickly as I had found it.

Gunther was becoming adept at hiding things from me.

I wasn't sure I liked it.

"I'm fine, I'm sorry," he said, his voice clear and strong again. He waved his hands as if magically banishing his admission and the lightning bolts of despair. "I have my mother back, I've been made ringmaster, my father and mother have been reunited. Despite the circumstances, I have little to despair about. Though I share your concern for your friend."

The energy that surrounded Gunther was now disciplined, compassionate, at ease. No storms within him. His usual steady nature rippled placidly against my interloper poking.

"You'd tell me if something was wrong, wouldn't you?"

There was a long pause.

"Of course, Charlotte."

As we passed through the outskirts of the town and the view out our windows turned to plains of scrub and grass, I was sure of a few things.

Tabitha's family was whacked.

The Avalon Grove Coven knew more about Tabitha than they were saying.

Gunther had just lied to me.

# CHAPTER 7

A STRANGE CAR WAS IN THE ANIMAL SHELTER
parking lot when we pulled up to my parents'.
Since the shelter itself closed at dusk, there
should be no cars here other than the ones my
family owns. As we parked, I glanced in to the
passenger window and spotted what looked like a
joystick in the car's center. "That's odd," I said.

"What's odd?"

"It must be for someone handicapped," I told
Gunther, spotting the blue placard hanging from
the rearview mirror.

"I'm not sure I understand." He leaned down
to peer in.

"If someone has an injury or illness that makes
it tougher for them to walk or drive, they get

things to aid them. I think that joystick-looking thing is one of those." I pointed. "The blue card with the person in the wheelchair? That means they can get a closer parking spot that allows for a wheelchair, some extra room to get in and out."

"That's a consideration I wouldn't have expected from a world that makes people pay for healing or suffer," Gunther observed as he stood back up.

"Hey, it's not the entire world," I said.

"Just this part of the world."

I walked toward the house without answering Gunther because, honestly, I didn't have an answer. One thing I loved about the Magical Midway was my ability to magic up what people needed without the worry it was taking away from someone else. Compared to our hippie lifestyle, the human world seemed...well, a little ruthless in some ways.

The human world was still better than the paranormal world—at least the world as ruled by fiat from Imperatorial City. You might not have to pay for healing there, but your family could get kidnapped and killed by the Witches' Council for expressing an opinion they didn't like. I wondered how Devana felt about *that* balance.

"Hey, it's not quite that bad," Gunther called as he jogged to catch up.

"Right, tell me about how you spent high school glowing like a light bulb to mark you as different, again?"

"They don't kidnap entire families, though," Gunther said. I pulled the screen door open. "Maybe *one* member as a warning, but not an *entire* family."

I rolled my eyes as we walked into the house.

Melissa Hayden sat on my parent's couch, her head twisting toward the entry hall as we came in. Resting against the end table was one shiny elbow crutch. There was no wheelchair in the room I could see.

"Charlotte," she smiled widely, greeting me like an old friend.

Grabbing the crutch, her arm flexed, and she rose with slow deliberateness from the sofa. Melissa wobbled like a newborn giraffe just learning how to manage its long, spindly legs. Beads of sweat broke out delicately across her brow with the effort.

"Melissa, you look fantastic!"

She did, no longer as pale as she was when I met her a few months ago. Her limbs looked stronger, more solid, and she had a light tan. Concern quickly overtook my happiness for her. The last time we were here, Gunther had healed Melissa Hayden. Aidan had told me it was a slower healing spell, one that would take years so as not to arouse suspicion.

*This* wasn't years.

*I didn't expect it to work this well,* Gunther thought sheepishly. *Well, I expected it to work well, but not fast. Not this fast.*

"You are my lucky charm, Charlotte." Melissa bowed her head. The college-aged girl sniffled as if she was holding back tears. "This all changed for me after Tiffany Drake's murder. More precisely, after you saved me from Anthony Drake."

"I didn't, really—"

"You did," she disagreed. "You saved me, and my life changed."

"Did it?"

"Yeah, almost immediately after." Melissa carefully lowered herself back down on the couch without looking up. "It's almost like God gave me back my legs as a reward for my brother killing that awful Anthony Drake, you know?"

"You think God did this?" Gunther asked. The corner of his mouth turned up, and I elbowed him. Hard.

"Well, I can't think of any other explanation for it, can you? The doctors swore that I would never walk again, and the pain stopped just a day before I felt the tingling in my legs." She leaned back and smiled widely. "The day I felt the tingling was the day that Micah…well, the day he did what needed to be done."

I didn't know what to say, so I nodded.

"Charlotte, I know that you're thrilled for Melissa's recovery, but she came here for a specific reason. Your friend Tabitha came to see her right after her brother killed Anthony Drake." My mother brought in a plate of cut-up fruit and placed it before Melissa on the coffee table. "They've become familiar acquaintances in the last few months."

"Yes, I'm sorry about getting distracted," Melissa, her eyes swimming with tears. "I get so excited about being able to walk, it sometimes takes over *everything* else that's happening."

"That's understandable," I said. I walked over to the chair and sat down to the right of Melissa Hayden. "I'm curious, since you and Tabitha are friends. Have you ever been to a store called Avalon Grove with her?"

"Sure I have!" She smiled and nodded. "Tabitha and I are in the outer circle of the Avalon coven."

"I don't understand what that means," I told her.

"Tabitha and I are not formal members of the coven," Melissa explained as she grabbed a grape from the plate in front of her. "There is an inner circle and an outer circle. The inner circle is made up of all the people that have been initiated under formal members of the coven. We're in the outer circle, so they allow us to go to some rituals, and the initiates teach us and guide us on stuff."

My stomach flexed with slightly amplified fear as Melissa explained her ties to Tabitha and the Avalon Grove. Samantha Goodfellow, the high priestess and proprietor of Avalon Grove, claimed Tabitha knew what my father was. Did that mean this girl did as well?

*She said there is no other explanation for what happened to her legs,* Gunther interjected telepathically. *Whatever Tabitha was looking into that concerned you, I don't think she shared it with this girl.*

At least not enough for her to put together the fact that a real paranormal witch healed her. Or that two of them sat in front of her. And one brought her a fruit and cheese plate.

"How does your brother feel about your friendship with Tabitha, and that you're into occult practices?" I asked Melissa casually. The girl might be sure that her brother had redeemed Anthony Drake's criminality by killing him, that the murder was some twisted form of altruism—but I was under no such illusions.

Michael Hayden's actions were the careful calculation of a sociopath fueled by greed and resentment. Nothing more.

"Oh, he's always got an opinion on everything," she waved her hand and rolled her eyes. "I don't pay any attention to him. I'm a grown-up and I can make my own decisions about my friends and my interests, thank you very much."

What a naïve girl. Being the sister of a gangster probably involved a certain ability to ignore things that one didn't want to know, but Melissa's total acceptance of her brother's nonexistent good nature seemed like a flashing neon sign pointing to an obvious suspect.

*You think Michael Hayden hurt Tabitha?*

Gunther asked. Kyle and Aidan walked in through the front door, their conversation stopping abruptly. I nodded almost imperceptibly to Gunther as Aidan reached out an arm to stop Kyle from issuing a cheerful greeting.

*So far, he's the only criminal we've come across who has previously murdered someone,* I thought back. *If it's always the Witches' Council in our world, here it seems like a safe bet that the rustic Mafia Godfather would be at the top of the suspect list.*

*You think Tabitha's been murdered?*

*I didn't say that! I—*

"Hey, are you the detective that investigated Tiffany Drake's murder?" Melissa pointed to the suddenly serious Kyle, his eyes scanning the room watching and listening. "You are, aren't you? You're that wimpy one that ran out of the room even though Anthony Drake had a gun pointed at me," she frowned.

Aidan grabbed his boyfriend's arm while a stormy expression gathered on the ex-detective's face. Low murmurs and angry whispers between Kyle and Aidan slowly faded as he yanked the angry centaur down the hall. Gunther straightened with a sigh, gesturing back toward Melissa.

"Melissa, what do you think happened to Tabitha?"

"Oh, right, that's actually what I came here to tell you." She jolted upright, her eyes wide. "I don't think *anything* happened to Tabitha at all."

I blinked in surprise. "You don't?"

"I don't," she shook her head no.

"What makes you say that?"

"I saw her dad at Pocket Burgers last night," she kneaded her knees with her fingers distractedly. "He was perfectly friendly, and when I asked about what I saw on the news? He waved it away and said they didn't know what they were talking about. That Tabitha was fine."

"He did?" Gunther caught my eye, and I saw the surprise in his face. *Didn't you go talk to her father?*

*Yes, and that's not the story we heard.*

"How often have you met Mr. Stevens, Melissa?"

"Oh, I don't know, maybe two or three times? Rarely, really," she shrugged. "I was super surprised that he recognized me enough to say hi. I didn't think he even knew who I was."

∾

Kyle looked at me sourly when Gunther and I went into the kitchen. "I'm not in the habit of letting anyone call me a coward," he snapped. His eyes flashed with indignation. "Not when I was a cop, and certainly not now that I'm a centaur."

"Look, no offense? I get that you have some kind of machismo uber-male thing going on here? But I can't explain to that girl that Gunther put you in a trance to force you to leave because I was bulletproofed." I tapped on my chest hard enough to produce the telltale clink. "We're back in the human world, dude. Lots of stuff we cannot explain."

"You don't live in this world anymore, Kyle," Aidan's hand gently squeezed Kyle's shoulder. "What these people think of you? It doesn't matter anymore."

"It matters," he grumbled. He crossed his arms and looked out the back window.

Aidan turned back and rolled his eyes.

"I heard that," Kyle snapped.

"Heard what?"

"Aidan's eye roll."

"You can hear an eye roll?" I asked incredulously.

"No, but I didn't have to hear it. I could *hear* it," he said.

Since Aidan was an accountant and Kyle was an ex-cop, I thought Aidan was the more sensitive person in this couple. It was clear from this exchange that I was wrong.

"Is Melissa still here?" Aidan asked, continuing to rub Kyle's tense neck consolingly. The distant sound of dogs happily barking and chasing one another through the play area seem to comfort Kyle. His taut shoulders slowly dropped from around his neck.

"Yeah, I think I'll invite her to go out to dinner with us," I told him as I gestured out the window toward the setting sun. "I don't want to question her in a formal way or anything, but I think getting her in an informal setting and just letting her talk? That might help."

"How so?" Kyle asked.

"She's friends with Tabitha. As far as she's concerned, I'm just another friend of Tabitha's," I told them. "Maybe if we take her out to dinner, she'll let something slip."

"We going for Italian food?" Gunther asked as he walked in.

"You mean Anthony Drake's old place?"

"I mean Michael Hayden's current place." Gunther draped an arm over my shoulder.

"Melissa just let me know her brother shut down Anthony Drake's crooked legal practice."

"Well, that's good, at least," I said. Anthony Drake's legal practice wasn't really a legal practice. It was more like a criminal practice where the head criminal happen to have a law degree. "Maybe Melissa is right and her sociopathic brother has had an attack of conscience."

"I wouldn't count on it." Gunther's right eyebrow shot up. "He works out of the Italian restaurant now, and he's become an oregano distributor. Mexican oregano, to be specific."

"He sells herbs?" Kyle asked suspiciously.

"Millions of dollars worth, apparently." Gunther nodded. "Melissa related that he's often gone at night because that's when the deliveries come in. It's a special Mexican herb, you see," Gunther smiled wryly. "Sunlight can damage it."

"That doesn't sound like any oregano I know," I told him.

Kyle glanced at me curiously and then rolled his eyes.

"What?" I asked him. "The sun doesn't hurt dried oregano. Heck, you can even get sun-dried oregano."

"He knows, Charlotte," Gunther patted me on

the back as if I were a child. "He knows it's not oregano. So do I. I think only you and Melissa still think he's shipping oregano."

"He's a pot dealer, dear," my mother said casually. She pushed through our crowd to get to her sink. "Michael Hayden gets tons of marijuana from Mexico and then distributes it to different dealers from his restaurant."

"Isn't that stuff legal already?" I asked my mom.

"This is Texas, dear. We don't do things like that here," she said as she washed the plates.

"Now, Martha, that's not quite the case," my father said, coming in through the back door. "Our government made that one dispensary so that the folks with medical issues could buy it."

"One, Alan. One in the entire state. Have you checked the map lately? One in a state as large as ours? I wouldn't even call that a baby step," Mom scoffed.

"Well, Martha, it's at least a crawl in the right direction." He kissed the back of her neck with a loud smack.

"Do we really think now is the time to discuss Texas politics and the legalization of marijuana?" I asked with a small amount of exasperation. "Tabitha is still missing and we're no closer to knowing what happened to her than we were this morning when we got here."

"You were the one having the little meeting in the kitchen, dear." My mother turned off the faucet and flung the excess water into the sink. Drying her hands with a hand towel, she turned to face me and continued. "No one is stopping you from getting in your car and going to Michael Hayden's restaurant, are they?"

"We haven't even decided to go to the restaurant. I don't know if taking Melissa to where her brother runs an illegal business is the smartest thing for us to do."

"Can you think of anything smarter?" Kyle asked me. "We have to eat, and you want to visit where Tabitha went missing at about the same time she would have gone. That's not for another two and a half hours yet."

"Do you really think Michael Hayden might have hurt Tabitha because he didn't like her influence on his sister?" Gunther asked me seriously.

Gunther's ability to rummage through the thoughts in my head was sometimes useful. I hadn't even plotted out that Hayden was someone I suspected, but he read all the shades of my questions and came up with one distinct hypothesis. A hypothesis that made me shudder.

"I don't know," I told him after thinking for a few seconds. "It's just...I mean, there's a crime and a criminal and a motive."

"We don't know yet that there is a crime," Aidan pointed out. "Melissa seem to think Mr. Stevens wasn't too concerned. Tabitha's been angry at both of us so if she went off somewhere...I mean, it's not like she would contact us."

"Wouldn't she contact her parents?" I asked him. "I know that Melissa thought he seemed unconcerned, but—"

"Honestly, when you and I met him? He didn't seem too concerned then, either." The two of us stared at each other in silence remembering the visit to the Stevenses'.

Gunther spoke up after a pause. "It sounded, though, that he was much more friendly to Melissa. Almost casual."

"I don't think she said enough for us to get that impression, Gunther. She really didn't go into it much."

"That would be a great thing to talk about at dinner," Kyle's mouth twitched into a smile.

# CHAPTER 8

"*Il Pirata?*" I asked. The bright red and green neon sign in front of the restaurant elicited peals of laughter from Kyle. The centaur was laughing so hard he had to lean against the Mediterranean columns for support. Tears rolled down his handsome face and Aidan's eyes widened. "What does that mean? *What's* so funny?"

"He changed the name of the restaurant to 'the pirate.' That's what the name of the place is. In Italian. Just '*the pirate.*' If I were still a cop struggling against the deep corruption in this town, that would probably infuriate me,." Kyle pointed. Then he shrugged and laughed. "I'm not, though, and I find the name of this restaurant utterly hilarious."

"At least Mr. Hayden has developed a sense of self-confidence and irony about his situation." Aidan gestured toward the parking lot. "His sister's headed this way, though, so I would suggest you get yourself under control. It's clear she believes her brother to be nothing more than a small-town restaurateur."

A few more chuckles worked their way out of Kyle, the last trailing off when Melissa joined us by the door.

"Don't you *love* what he's done with the place?" she asked, her eyes twinkling as they swept across the bright facade. "It was so dingy and depressing before, old and cracked and…It looked like no one really took care, you know? Michael worked hard to brighten up the place, and I think he did a great job." Melissa beamed with pride and looked at us expectantly.

We murmured the required compliments. The sociopathic murderer had good taste.

Truthfully, Melissa wasn't kidding about her brother making changes. As we pushed in the restaurant, I noticed the deep, dark wood panels that previously covered the interior of the restaurant from floor to ceiling were gone. In their place were bright, whitewashed walls with green and red accents along the molding. Hayden had installed big bay windows on all three sides of the dining area allowing a flood of light from outside that brightened what used to be a dingy interior. He had also removed the separate rooms for seating so *Il Pirata* was one large open, airy parlor.

"I have to admit—this is nice," Gunther said as he leaned over. "I didn't really expect something this bright and airy to be designed by a—"

"Non-Italian?" Michael Hayden stepped in front of us. The young, plain-looking felonious crime boss scrutinized our group, his gaze travelling from person to person. "I wasn't expecting to see *you* back in my town so soon," Michael said without ceasing his shark-like scan of each of us. "Though with the situation going on, I suppose I *shouldn't* be surprised."

"Michael!" Melissa said as she moved out from behind Kyle. "You can be friendlier than *that*."

It was like watching a coiled snake poised to strike morph into a guarded but cordial German Shepherd. Michael Hayden didn't go from murderous to friendly, but he went from murderous and suspicious to…well, slightly less murderous and suspicious. The lines in his face softened as his sister made her way toward him, and one corner of his mouth turned up in a half smile.

"Melissa, it's good to see you." Michael embraced her. "What are you doing with *this* lot? Are they harassing you about this Tabitha woman?" With Melissa in his arms, Hayden shot me a look of anger over the slight girl's shoulder. It was gone as soon as he pulled away.

"What? No, *I* went to go see Charlotte, Micah. Sheesh, you are so suspicious sometimes. I swear, I don't know where you get it from." The girl rolled her eyes. "Tabitha talked about Charlotte *all the time*, you know. As soon as somebody told me the circus was over by her parents' house I rushed over there hoping I could make sure Charlotte wasn't worried."

"If Charlotte is concerned about Tabitha, she has every right to be worried, Mel," he told her. Michael glared at me again. "The young lady is missing."

I glared back.

"Harley, can you get my sister and her group a table toward the back, please? Then bring out two plates of steamed mussels and make sure Tony knows they're for Melissa and her…friends."

"Right away, Mr. Hayden," Harley, a cute blonde, smiled widely. She blushed, and I felt the attraction she had for her dangerous boss flare. Some women just had no common sense with men. I glanced over at Gunther and was grateful again that I could find someone in this world as kind and compassionate as he was.

"If you will all follow Harley, I need to see about a few things and then I'll join you," Hayden said still, eyeing me. Melissa slid him a curious glance and then shrugged, turning away to follow the waitress. "I could use a break in the day."

My eyes narrowed.

"That's all right, isn't it?" Hayden asked with a raised eyebrow. The man who shot and killed someone right in front of me, right in front of his sister…that man stared at me with an expression that wasn't predatory, but wasn't quite…not. "I wouldn't want to ruin any plans you have, Ms. Astley."

"It is your restaurant, I suppose you can sit anywhere you like, Mr. Hayden," I responded casually.

"Yes, I suppose I can at that." The two of us stared at one another for a good five seconds before Gunther leaned closer and draped his arm around me protectively.

Michael Hayden let out a sharp laugh and turned away.

"I don't like him," Gunther whispered as we sat in the soft leather booth. Melissa chatted with her brother, her eyes shining, her lips curled into a smile. I felt frustrated. Someone may have hurt Tabitha, she could be dead, she could be captured somewhere and held against her will. What were we doing? Waiting for the lasagna.

*I don't know why you would like him,* I thought to Gunther in response to his whispered statement. *He's a drug dealer, he's a murderer, and even if he wasn't any of those things? He has all the charm of a bear trap waiting to spring shut on your leg.*

Gunther nodded and frowned. Gunther Makepeace and Michael Hayden were as opposite as two men could be. Gunther was warm and caring and gentle. Michael Hayden's energy was cold and controlled. If Gunther was a soft teddy bear, Michael was a razor-sharp knife. There *was* nothing to like about the man.

As if he picked up vibrations from my thoughts, Hayden turned.

"I take it you have returned to our humble little town because of Tabitha Stevens' disappearance?"

"My mother let me know she was missing while we were on the tour," I told him. "We got back as soon as we could."

"I understood that Ms. Stevens was no longer a friend of yours, Ms. Astley." Hayden nodded toward his sister. "Why were you concerned enough to return to Mickwac?"

"Because she's my friend," I told him coldly. Maybe Michael Hayden *couldn't* understand why someone would care about someone else even if that someone else was upset with them. Sociopathic monsters probably didn't care about people unless those people were useful to them.

"I told Charlotte that Tabitha is probably fine," Melissa announced cheerfully to the table, oblivious to the tension between her brother and me. "Mr. Stevens didn't seem concerned at all about where Tabitha was last night when I saw him at Pocket Burgers. I bet she went off camping in the woods or something."

"Does she do that a lot?" Kyle asked. "Solo camping trips?"

"I don't know that she does it a *lot*," she answered. "She's gone on like three or four trips on her own. The last time was two months ago. I offered to go with her but she said she wanted to use the time for meditation and bonding with the land."

"What did she mean by 'bonding' with the land?" Aidan asked.

"It's just a phrase we use at Avalon Grove," Melissa shrugged. Her brother looked sharply at her. "It means nothing specific. It's just, like, learning to be one with nature and stuff. Tree-hugging, I guess? I don't know, I go to Galveston to become one with nature. I like bonding with the beach better."

Harley appeared at the head of our table and displayed a bottle of wine to Michael. Once he nodded, she poured a small glass for everyone and then backed away quickly, leaving us alone again.

"I need to wash my hands," Melissa said waving her hand toward her brother. "Scoot out, let me run to the bathroom." Michael Hayden slid out of the booth with one liquid movement and turned immediately to assist. "I *got* it, Michael. It's fine." she reached for her single crutch, waving him away.

"You can still accept help, you know," he told her.

"If I don't need it, no reason to take it." With a

smile, she ambled slowly toward the back of the restaurant.

"Keep my sister out of this," Hayden told me coldly.

"I didn't go talk to *her*," I said as his eyes bored into my own. "She came to see *me*, remember?"

"As I told you once before, I am grateful that you helped to protect my sister when the Drakes were a threat to her, but that goodwill only goes so far." He glanced toward the back of the restaurant. "This situation with your friend Tabitha is far more complicated than you know, and it's far more dangerous. I don't want Melissa anywhere near it."

"What do you mean, it's far more dangerous?" I asked him. "You know something about what happened to her, don't you?"

"I know nothing directly about what happened to Tabitha Stevens, no," Hayden answered, his eyes darting again toward the back of the restaurant. "I know about Darius Stevens, however. Considering Mr. Stevens has similar ambitions to my own, I've made it a priority to keep tabs on the man."

"Ambitions like yours? What does that mean?" Gunther asked Michael, his voice low.

"It is the nature of the game." Hayden lowered

his voice and leaned forward. "As I once sought to displace Anthony Drake on the ladder of accomplishments, so, too, does Darius Stevens wish to make that climb himself."

"Wait a minute," I said, shooting him a look of disbelief. "Are you saying that Darius Stevens is a criminal—"

"I am saying that Darius Stevens is not who he pretends to be to the outside world," Michael Hayden interrupted as he crossed his arms. "I am who I am, and I don't pretend to be otherwise. Darius Stevens pretends to be a respected businessman, someone who is self-made and who has resources accumulated through his own technical talent in the biomedical field. While he is that, he is also much more."

"Are you saying—" Kyle tried to interject, but Michael Hayden cut him off.

"Darius Stevens is a hacker," he interrupted. "Your former colleagues are defensive regarding any interference or attention from federal law enforcement, and so Mr. Stevens has amassed quite a stockpile of resources to do whatever he wishes. What he wishes now is to displace me in Mickwac."

"Why?" I asked him.

"Why else? Power," he said. "I've known of his

machinations for some years, but it wasn't until Tabitha investigated your disappearance with Avalon Grove that Darius Stevens' ambitions for control of this town matched my own in intensity. He realized something—what, I don't know—that made him believe strongly in his own ability to achieve and maintain power."

"Why are you telling me this?" I asked him suspiciously. "You barely know me, and this doesn't seem like a smart conversation to be having with someone out in the open in the middle of your restaurant, much less with someone who—"

"Could turn me in to the police?" he asked, his eyebrow raising. "I'm sure your friend over here could explain to you how ineffective that would be. Even if you recorded this exchange, Ms. Astley, giving it to the police department for action would be more than futile."

"If he has the same protections that Anthony Drake had? He's right," Kyle assured me. "He has most of the police department on the payroll, most likely."

"Okay, why, then? Why tell me all this?"

"My sister still doesn't know what I do for a living," Hayden said and his eyes flashed at me. "I would like to keep it that way for as long as possible. Unfortunately, that means when she gets herself involved in situations I would prefer she not, it's challenging for me to protect her."

"What does that have to do with us?" Gunther asked him. Hayden refused to acknowledge that Gunther had asked any question at all and continued his relentless focus on me. The glint in his dark eyes was mesmerizing as if Hayden practiced staring and holding people's attention, and I focused on it waiting for him to continue.

"She told me what Tabitha believed your father to be." He continued staring, a faint smile played about his lips. "While Melissa shrugged off the story as impossible, I know what my sister's prognosis was. I know that she should not be walking."

Shivers ran down my spine.

"Well, then it's good a miracle happened," I said as my face reddened.

"Yes, an unexpected miracle happened," Hayden said leaning back. "Unexpected for Melissa, perhaps. I suspect her recovery was not so unexpected to you, Ms. Astley."

"I don't know what you mean," I told him, pulled my eyes away, and shrugged. "I barely know Melissa. I know nothing about her medical prognosis."

"I didn't expect you to admit anything, Ms. Astley, and I'm not telling you I know what happened to force you into some kind of confession. We all have our secrets," he said. Kyle, Aidan and Gunther stared at Michael Hayden, each working to feign a look unconcerned with the conversation. They were working *so hard* to look unconcerned that the tension was palpable. "I am letting you know because I *expect* you to protect my sister and to keep her as far away from the situation as you can."

"If *you* can't control your sister, I don't know how you expect that *I* can."

"No?" Hayden asked, a smile playing about his lips. "I suspect you have methods at your disposal I do not. And I expect you to use them."

"Not here—" I began, when Gunther kicked me under the table. "Ow!"

*What are you doing?* Gunther thought angrily. *This guy is as bad as the Witches' Council in his own way. Do you want to give him information like that? That your powers are not as strong off the Fairgrounds?*

*Do we care if the Witches' Council kills Michael Hayden for knowing about us?*

Gunther didn't respond.

"Look, Mr. Hayden—"

"Ah, Charlotte, call him Michael! Or Micah." Melissa plopped down next to her brother in the booth and grabbed her glass of wine. "With everything that Tabitha has told me about you, honestly, I feel like we're friends *already*."

Melissa's disposition was like the sun coming out from behind the cloud that was her brother. Cheerful, friendly and open, she was the opposite of her brother in almost every way I had noticed. In another life, at another time she and I *might* have been friends. It didn't surprise me that Tabitha had become one.

"Melissa, Charlotte won't be here long. Don't get too attached to her," Michael warned.

"She's not a puppy you won't let me keep, Micah." She balled up her fist and lightly punched her brother. "There're phones, there is email, and Charlotte's parents are here, so I'm sure she'll be back often. I'm just saying, Tabitha talked about Charlotte so much that it feels like I know her."

Harley brought two large plates of mussels and gently set them down in the table's center. The split shells peeked out of the golden pools of butter, and my mouth watered at the scent. All the guys reached in and grabbed handfuls of steamy mollusks, but I hesitated. Just how much *did* Michael Hayden know about ringmasters?

Did he know the only way to kill us was through digestible poison we fed to ourselves?

He couldn't know that.

Right?

I stared longingly at the mollusks.

*Good point,* Gunther said as he released his handful back into the lake of melted butter whence they came and wiped his greasy hand on the white linen napkin. *In retrospect, eating at a murderer's restaurant wasn't the best idea for you and me.*

*Well, his sister's eating from the same shared plate,* I thought sullenly as my stomach growled. *Maybe it's fine.*

*Do you want to risk your life on a maybe?*

"Not hungry?" Hayden asked me, his eyebrow raised.

"Gunther and I ate already," I told him.

"No, you didn't—" Kyle started, but he stopped when Gunther kicked him under the table.

"Believe nothing you hear and only half of what you see," Hayden murmured as he stared at me.

"What's that supposed to mean?" Gunther asked him.

# CHAPTER 9

"I'm *starving*," I told the guys an hour later as we stood in the parking lot waiting for Melissa to finish saying goodbye to her sociopathic brother. "Before we drive out, I *have* to grab some food."

"Do you *really* think Hayden knows about poisoning ringmasters?"

"Well, if he didn't know about it before, I guess he does *now*," I told Kyle, glaring. I rarely unloaded on my friends, but I couldn't help it. I plowed ahead, unloading on Aidan's boyfriend loudly and using my hands to emphasize the point. I couldn't help it. I was seriously hungry, and it had seriously been his idea to eat here. "The parking lot is bugged, remember? Is there anything else you want to let them know while we're standing here? Any other paranormal secrets you want to broadcast to the criminal underbelly of Mickwac?"

I stomped my foot.

"Charlotte, I'm not sure you're helping the situation," Gunther said. Kyle raised his hands in surprise.

"Which situation is that?" I asked Gunther as I turned my peckish aggravation on him. "The situation with the sociopathic crime boss and the restaurant, the evil hacker aspiring to be a sociopathic crime boss that also happens to be the father of my missing friend, or the situation with the local human witches' coven?"

"The local human witches' coven? What do they have to do with this?" Gunther asked me.

"They know about us, too."

Gunther raised his eyebrow.

"Well, the coven leader implied that she knew what Charlotte was," Aidan told the group. Kyle glanced toward the door to see if Melissa was on her way. "Samantha Goodfellow never really *said* that anyone else knew what Charlotte was. Just that she did."

Gunther's expression hardened as he cast his eyes around the perimeter of the parking lot.

"That's an awful lot of people claiming to know what we are," he said quickly. Gunther glanced my way and I could see the concern reflecting in his eyes. "All this because your friend Tabitha saw your father make some animals behave? I don't buy it."

"What you mean?" Kyle asked him.

"There's nothing about your father's power that *proves* magic exists," Gunther pointed ou, leaning back against the truck. "No sparkles, nothing defying the law of physics. The animals don't suddenly speak like a human would. They don't do something an animal wouldn't normally do. He just says something or thinks something and animals listen and obey. A good animal trainer could do what he did. Maybe seeing ten or twenty dogs all sit when a human being says *sit* is peculiar, but it certainly is *explainable*."

"Okay, I see what you're saying," Kyle nodded, but he didn't sound convinced.

"I don't think you do," Gunther disagreed. "What Tabitha supposedly saw is *not* proof of the paranormal. Not at all. It's not convincing, it's not belief changing. So if that's not proof of the paranormal, what did she discover or that coven discover that's suddenly making everyone in your hometown believe in paranormals?"

"Everybody doesn't believe in paranormals—"

"Michael Hayden just implied *he* does," Gunther disagreed with me. "It sounds like Tabitha believed it. You said that Samantha Goodfellow believed it. Her son, Raven Goodfellow—that kid *certainly* seemed to believe it."

"We didn't mention him—" Aidan began.

"Assume that anything Charlotte sees I might have seen," Gunther told him. "And I have to say that young man disturbed me enough that I almost left Kyle and headed over. He had an unhealthy interest in Charlotte."

"I again need to point out that we're talking in a parking lot that might be bugged," I told the group with exasperation.

"Frankly, Charlotte, whoever's listening probably knows more than we do about what's going on in this town." Kyle ran his hand through his hair and sighed. "The police wouldn't be listening in Michael Hayden's parking lot."

"Why not?"

"They didn't have the parking lot bugged when Anthony Drake owned the place," Kyle told me. "One of the cops I saw today told me that Hayden pays better than Drake ever did."

"Good to know," I told him.

I wanted to make some snappy, sarcastic response but the whole situation just struck me as ridiculously sad. This town and the people in it didn't deserve to be the epicenter of a metrosexual Mafia war or a paranormal conspiracy. Gunther leaned in and pressed his cheek against my forehead.

*The town doesn't seem any worse for the wear, Gunther thought.*

"How can you say that?" I snapped at him out loud, pushing him away. "Tabitha's missing and the police aren't even looking for her! That's *not* worse for the wear?"

"I'm sorry, Charlotte, I didn't mean—"

"Forget it," I told Gunther looking toward the door of *Il Pirata*. "Melissa's coming out—"

Before I could finish my sentence, Tabitha's face danced before my eyes and my skin was on fire. I felt like a soda pop bottle someone had shaken up, energy pressed against all sides of me from the inside and I gasped for air. With an explosion of light behind my eyes, everything went dark and I heard my head bounce off the asphalt as I hit the parking lot ground with a loud metal clank.

〜

"Charlotte! Charlotte!" Gunther shouted. I could feel his hands clasped around my face and his thumbs pressing into my cheeks. Because of our ringmaster shielding, Gunther's touch produced annoying tinny clangs that echoed in my ears. "I think she's coming back around. Charlotte, can you hear me?"

I fluttered my eyelids and looked up at the three men fanned out around me, each forehead creased with concern. "I'm all right," I mumbled, pushing away from the truck tire they had leaned me against. I shuddered to think what my clothing must look like from behind. "Back up, you guys. I'm fine."

"You are *not* fine," Gunther disagreed. Aidan opened his mouth to agree but Kyle cut him off.

"I don't care *what* that huntress witch said, normal people don't just pass out," Kyle said as he reached out for my right arm. Aidan grabbed my left and Gunther continued to maintain contact with my face. "How do we even know she could be trusted, anyway? If Devana had found something, would she have bothered to tell us? Or would she just run and tell Ethel Elkins, leaving you in the dark?"

"Do we not have enough problems right now?" I asked Kyle and stood up firmly. "In case you haven't noticed, Kyle, I'm anything but *normal.* Can't we just deal with the issues in front of us?"

"A minute ago the issue in front of us was *you.* On the *ground.*" Kyle released my arm.

Brushing the dust off my pants, I glared at the three men. "Where's Melissa?" I asked them, looking up.

"She ran back inside to call an ambulance," Kyle said, his eyes widening. I glared at the centaur. He sighed. "I'll go get her." With wide strides, he ran like a shot toward the door. Turning back toward Gunther, I noticed my boyfriend stood perfectly still with his arms crossed. His face was still deeply creased with concern.

"What?"

"Don't *what* me," Gunther snapped. I jumped as his accusatory stare paired itself with a lightning bolt of frustration that exploded in my direction. "Just because you've got used to being mostly indestructible doesn't mean you're *completely* indestructible. This *is* concerning, Charlotte."

"It's concerning to *you.*" I turned toward the truck and fixed my hair using my reflection in the car window. My hand trembled as I fluffed the static layers away from my face. but I was determined not to show Gunther any fear. "Look, people faint. It's probably just concern for Tabitha, just the stress. We have other things we need to focus on, and Devana already checked me out, remember?"

"I remember," he said. "You remember I can literally slip into your mind, correct? Whatever you're trying to hide from me? You're not hiding it."

"What's got into you?" I whirled to face him, my eyes narrowing. "You've been snippy with me all day."

"No, I *really* haven't," Gunther told me with a half smile. "You're actually the one snipping at me, Charlotte. For some reason, you seem to think that my concern isn't valid."

"You do have a habit of projecting sometimes, Charlotte," Aidan agreed unhelpfully.

"Look, Gunther, I just don't want to get distracted," I told him, ignoring Aidan. "Each time it's happened, I see Tabitha's face in front of mine and her mouth is open as if she's screaming, but I can't *hear* anything. I really do just think that I'm worried. I don't want you being worried about me being worried about Tabitha to distract from actually finding her."

"That was kind of hard to follow," Aidan said cocking his head.

"Stop helping me, bestie," I told him without turning around. Aidan rolled his eyes and lifted his hands up in submission.

Gunther's arms continued to be crossed, but his face softened as he considered me. "Look, I don't want you to push me away, Charlotte. I understand that you are afraid for your friend, and I understand that you fear something may have happened to her, but *you* need to understand that *my* primary concern is *you*. That won't change."

"I know." I glared.

"Don't lie to me about how you feel."

"Okay," I grumbled. Then I glared some more.

"Because if you lie to me about how you feel, I'll know it,." Gunther walked forward and gathered me in his arms. "And if you are lying to me about how you feel? Lying to me about something being wrong? It's just going to make me more concerned."

*"Okay, I get it, I get it!"* Just the way I knew you were lying to me when you told me everything was okay at the Makepeace Circus.

If Gunther picked up on my thought, he didn't show it.

"There's the bridge," I told Aidan, pointing. It had taken us a half an hour to drive out here, after the fifteen minutes for us to separate ourselves from Melissa Hayden. I knew that she was just trying to be helpful, but I didn't entirely trust that her information was correct, and I didn't want her around while we examined the place where Tabitha's car was found. "Kyle, do you know which side of the bridge she was on? Her car, I mean."

"She was going north toward the city." Kyle pointed to the right. "We are going north, so she would've parked her car right over there."

Aidan pulled the car over and the rest of us jumped out of the vehicle before he even turned the engine off. "Charlotte, do you know if your father keeps any flashlights in the truck?"

"Check the tool chest in the back," I told him. He nodded.

Aside from the occasional hoot of an owl and the rustle of the trees in the wind, the rural area we had driven to was quiet. A little too quiet, almost. As if the area was holding its breath waiting for us to arrive. The calmness of the countryside felt much more like tension than peace.

"Can you feel that?" Gunther asked quietly.

"There is magic here," Aidan murmured as he swung his head around and scanned the trees on either side of the road. "Not *right* here, mind you but...It's close. I can feel it."

"What you mean, you can *feel* it?" I asked him.

"You can't?" Aidan asked, surprised.

I closed my eyes and breathed deeply trying to sense what both Gunther and Aidan had noticed that I had not. The world still felt quiet around me, with shuffling wildlife and a soft wind, but I couldn't *feel* magic—though to be honest, I wasn't sure what I was supposed to be looking for. I opened my eyes and shrugged at them both. "I don't know what I'm *supposed* to be feeling, but it just feels like an old country road to me."

"She's never been the most intuitive person," Aidan told Gunther.

"What on earth are you talking about? I'm a freaking empath and telepath, for goodness sake. I'm literally the *very definition* of an intuitive person," I disagreed, crossing my arms.

"Those are your *powers*, Charlotte," Gunther explained shaking his head. "Thoughts and emotions that other people have, those are things that you were born to read and understand. Intuition is the ability to understand something without the need for consciously reading it. You read people, yes, but sometimes you have trouble understanding things that are not completely obvious."

"What Gunther's trying to say," Aidan jumped in as he read the anger creeping up my cheeks. "Is that you've never really had to develop your intuition. You're very pragmatic, and you're very smart. But people have never been able to hide things from you, and so you've never really had to wonder what's beneath their motivation."

"You spot things that people show you, and that people tell you. You can piece together a story from all of that." Kyle handed each one of us a flashlight. "When you have the ability to see *that* much of a situation, you don't have to guess. I doubt you've ever been in a situation where you weren't a hundred percent sure of what everyone was doing and feeling."

"It's always been easy for you," Gunther smiled. "That's not a bad thing. Your problem has always been having too much information, though."

"Our problem has been never having enough," Aidan explained.

"Or having people lie," Kyle added. "The rest of us mere mortals have had to develop skills to suss out situations because we couldn't just pluck the facts from someone's mind."

"Okay, okay, I get it. I'm not intuitive. I don't notice that there's magic nearby," I told them sullenly. I turned away and walked toward the sloppy rectangle spray-painted on the concrete of the bridge. "I've had it super easy all my life because I knew what everyone around me was thinking and I never had to bother working at anything. Got it."

"Charlotte, that's *not* what we're saying," Aidan called. I kept walking away. "It's just that we're getting into situations where people are deliberately trying to keep things from you. That's a new situation for you and—"

Light exploded behind my eyes and my chest squeezed until I could hardly gasp for air. Tabitha's face glowed in front of me, her hands up with palms out pushing against the air in front of her. Her eyebrows knitted together with concern as her eyes bored into me. Her mouth moved rapidly as if she was trying to tell me something, but the only thing I heard was the hiss of energy.

I grabbed the bridge's rail, clutching it so

tightly that I was afraid my fingers would break. I stared at the image, determined to remain conscious through its onslaught. "Can you see that?" I shouted at the men, determined to figure out if Tabitha was in front of me or within my own mind.

"See what? Oh, no, not again!" Gunther shouted and I heard the pounding of feet.

"Don't touch me!" I wheezed, and then inhaled sharply. "Don't do anything to me! I have to understand what she's telling me!" Tabitha's head shook back and forth, and her face grew angry. She crossed her arms and rolled her eyes, bouncing up and down as if she stomped her foot. "I can't hear you! I can't hear anything you're saying! What are you trying to tell me?"

I gasped as her brow furrowed. She uncrossed her arms and held them up again on either side of her face, palms spread wide. She pushed forward again wildly, as if opening a heavy door. Tears sprang to my eyes and I shook my head no. "I don't understand you, Tabitha!"

The image of Tabitha threw her hands up and her eyes shot to the sky. She looked frustrated.

"Charlotte, you're turning *white*," Kyle said. I could feel all three of the guys almost touching me, but not quite. I knew they were there, and they filled up the space around me, waiting. "If you start to fall, we need to catch you—"

"Don't touch me!"

Suddenly Tabitha jumped up and down. She pointed to me, then made a motion like driving a car. I nodded because that was easy enough to understand. She smiled, then lifted her hand and motioned walking with her fingers. I nodded again. She pointed at me once more, made the walking motion, pointed at me again, and then shook her head no.

"I don't understand!"

She pointed at me again, made the walking motion, and then took that hand and slammed the walking person downward. Then she lifted both arms, extended them in front of her and pushed them wide with her palms out over and over again. Then she pointed at me, and drew her finger across her neck. She stopped and looked at me hopefully.

I shook my head no, a hot flood of anger painting Tabitha's image red in my mind. "You want me to drive somewhere and not walk? Is that it?"

Her face fell in disappointment.

Then she disappeared.

～

"You think that she's trying to communicate with you? That's what these attacks have been?" Gunther asked, his hand gently pressing against my shoulder. "I thought she was human?"

"There are some humans with telepathic ability," Aidan said.

"I don't think that's what this is," I disagreed. Sitting on the bridge, I struggled to make sense of the communication I just had with Tabitha Stevens. Clearly she was trying to tell me something, and it didn't seem like it was about rescuing her. "I couldn't hear her, and if it was telepathy I would've been able to hear what she was saying or read her somehow. I couldn't. It was like playing a game where I had to guess what she was telling me just from her movements."

"You're sure she was alive?" Kyle asked. My eyes narrowed. "Look, we *are* paranormals, and she *could* have been a ghost. I'm just trying to get as much information as we can."

"She was alive," I told him, sitting back. "I know you guys think I'm not intuitive at all and I can't put anything together without a *big neon sign* flashing in my face, but she was alive. I've talked to ghosts before, and she was no ghost."

Kyle paced slowly in front of me while Aidan and Gunther sat cross-legged on either side of me. The four of us gathered just inches from the police outline of Tabitha's now-absent impounded car. "She made motions for driving, for walking, for me not to go walking, she pressed her palms out over and over. Then the universal signal for being decapitated."

"Humans are decapitated so often that there is a universal signal for it?" Gunther asked.

"Not really," Kyle told him distractedly without ceasing his pacing. "It's just become a way to get across a risk of death, or to make a joke about killing someone."

"A joke? About killing someone?" Gunther asked, surprised.

"Dude, witches made you glow like a light bulb in high school," I told Gunther. "Every species has their weirdness, ours isn't any better or worse than yours."

"You mean the *humans'* weirdness is not any better or worse than *ours*," Gunther said. I stared at him.

"Can we get back to the issue at hand?" Kyle

snapped in our direction. He stopped pacing and held out his hand. I grabbed it and allowed him to pull me up. "Maybe it's the ex-cop in me but when someone tells me not to do something? That's usually the first thing I want to do."

"What do you mean?" Aidan asked.

"Tabitha told Charlotte not to go walking." Kyle waved the flashlight. "So, I think we should go walking."

"But Tabitha told her not to," Gunther said.

"The fact that Tabitha told Charlotte *anything* at all makes me suspect that Tabitha's ability to communicate with Charlotte and get through to her relies a lot on Charlotte's proximity to where Tabitha is right now," Kyle told Gunther. "If that's true, Tabitha's likely being held somewhere close to this spot. Probably somewhere in the hills on either side of us."

"Why wouldn't she want Charlotte to go look for her?"

"Maybe she hasn't been kidnapped." Kyle began slowly pacing again, his eyes scanning the tree line once more. "Maybe she's doing something that she doesn't want Charlotte to find out about. Maybe she has been kidnapped and she's afraid Charlotte would get hurt."

"She doesn't know that Charlotte's indestructible," Aidan snapped his fingers.

"Exactly," Kyle nodded. "She could be trying to protect her friend not realizing—"

"That I don't need her protection," I finished. "I don't need *anyone's* protection."

Gunther glanced over at me, a bland expression on his face as he worked hard to suppress any outward reaction to my statement. I could feel in my non-intuitive, rules-breaking brain a telepathic wound that bled ever so slightly within him. Kyle and Aidan glanced at one another.

"In any case," Kyle said, pointing toward a path that snaked into the scrubby hill on the opposite side of the bridge, "that looks well-traveled, which means it leads somewhere." I turned and leaned over the side of the bridge we stood upon and looked to either side of the bank. Though it was dark, the streetlights illuminated the muddy banks of the creek.

"Can y'all see any paths on this side?" I asked.

"Did you just say *y'all*?" Gunther asked.

"You are *much* more easily distracted than I remember," I told him without turning around.

"I don't see anything on this side, at least

nothing as defined as that path across the way," Aidan said.

Kyle agreed, and the four of us made our way across the two-lane bridge toward the curved track, flashlights in hand.

# CHAPTER 10

"You know, if the situation weren't so dire this would be a nice hike," Gunther said. He swept his flashlight deep into the brush along the ground. "It's a little dusty and dry, but the land is interesting."

"I've never exactly been a hiking kind of girl," I responded as I swept the opposite side of the path. "Texas land is pretty from a distance, I'll grant you that. But it can be an itchy and stinging experience if you're not careful."

Gunther laughed quietly. We followed behind Aidan and Kyle over uneven ground. Ascending carefully and deliberately up the gently-sloped hill, I strained to hear any sounds in the dusty wilderness that didn't quite belong. Despite

Aidan's claim I wasn't very intuitive, I could sense things slithering and creeping quietly all around me as the creatures of the night hunted for their dinner.

"They stopped," Gunther pointed his light at the feet of the two men ahead of us. The two had reached the top of the hill and stared out over the expanse at something.

"What is it?" I asked. We climbed up the last few feet swiftly, so swiftly that as I walked around Kyle to stand beside him, my foot slipped off the sheer cliff in front. I felt it throw off my center of gravity as I tumbled forward.

"I've got her!" Kyle shouted and his strong hands yanked me back. "Maybe move a *little* slower next time, Ringmaster? You'll probably bounce, but the clanging ruckus your shields would make will probably attract unwanted attention. If the invisible weight of it didn't pull you down below the water."

"Thanks for your concern," I pushed him away and pulled my shirt straight.

"What *is* this place?" Gunther asked as his flashlight cast about the thick grove of tall trees.

We stood on the edge of a clearing hundreds of feet across, a gaping hole of emptiness we sensed more than saw. As our flashlights scanned the area below, jade green water reflected the beams back to us. We were staring into some kind of underground grotto, the faint sound of a water dripping breaking the silence.

"Step back," Kyle warned. "The roof of this place is limestone, and the circled opening?" Kyle's flashlight scanned the edge of the huge pool, shining a light on the gigantic boulders piled around the emerald water. "I think that was made when the roof collapsed into the cave."

"The pathway leads right here, though." Aidan looked around. He walked back a few steps and shined his flashlight along the path we had just climbed. "How do you get in?"

We all scanned and searched but found nothing. Back at the ledge peering in, Kyle was the first one to make a suggestion.

"Jump?" Kyle asked.

"If you do that, how do you get *out*?" Aidan asked.

The four of us stood at the edge of the grotto opening and swept our flashlights along the edge of the pool. I had lived here all of my life and had never heard of this place, a place that surely would have been a swimming hole during the hot Texas summers. Every swimming hole in Texas eventually became legendary, directions shared and posted online so others could enjoy.

Whether it was a formal swimming hole or a secret one that people snuck onto someone's property to use, something like this would never have remained hidden for long.

"Maybe we—"

Whatever Kyle's idea might have been, none of us got to hear it. Before he could get from one end of his sentence to another, the ground beneath our feet pulled away, and we tumbled into the open maw of darkness.

"Everybody okay?" Gunther called from somewhere to my right. I reached my hands out frantically, slapping the water in the darkness as I tried to grasp anyone who might have been near me. My hands touched nothing, and the emptiness was oppressive.

"I'm okay. Wet, but okay," Kyle called from my left. "Aidan?"

Silence.

"Aidan!"

The silence was deafening for a few seconds as we all stilled to listen. After four seconds, bursts of splashing came from either side of me. I thrust my hands out and swept in wide arcs hoping my hand would connect with Aidan, but I didn't. I could feel nothing but water, and my eyes only saw inky blackness. The water was warm, comforting almost, despite the precarious position I found myself in.

"Aidan, are you here? Answer me!" Kyle's voice rose in volume. I could hear the panic just underneath struggling to break out. It tinged his strong police officer gruffness with an edge of fear.

"I'm here," Aidan called weakly. His voice sounded tight, and it came from far away.

"Where are you?" Gunther called into the darkness.

"I think...I think...I'm on a rock...I don't know if it's on the side or in the water's middle...I can't...I can't move my arms to feel anything..." he said in gasps. "My legs feel...My legs feel odd."

"Keep talking, Aidan, just keep speaking so I can find you," Kyle said. I heard more methodical splashing and assumed Kyle was swimming toward Aidan's voice.

I floated toward it myself while treading water. I didn't worry about Gunther, and it was clear when I heard the second person swimming toward Aidan he wasn't worrying about me. There were benefits to being ringmasters and having inherent protections against damage.

They were benefits that Kyle and Aidan did not enjoy.

A glowing orb flared twenty feet to my right. It barely illuminated the darkness I was feeling lost in, but it was just enough I could faintly see Aidan clutching a slab that jutted out diagonally from the water.

"I've got you," Kyle whispered, but his voice echoed within the cavern so I heard him. I could see the shadow of the centaur as he scrambled up on the rock next to Aidan. His hand extended and as it connected with Aidan's shoulder, my friend let out a moan. "It hurts that bad, huh? I barely touched you."

"It hurts," Aidan responded.

"Can't you heal him? Either one of you?" Kyle called out.

"I can try," Gunther said. He pulled himself out of the water and balanced on the bottom edge of the slippery rock. "As long as it's not too complicated, if it's just mending bones or nerves, I should be able to make it better than it is now. Soft tissue damage, though, is tricky."

As I watched Gunther concentrate, I kicked

myself for not paying more attention to the lessons I'd abandoned months ago because of the prophecy. Without my ringmaster powers I was a fairly incompetent witch. Gunther may have hated attending the schools in Impy, but the education he had came in handy frequently.

"Do you think the roof just wasn't strong enough to hold us?" I asked Kyle while Gunther worked to heal the damaged Aidan. "I didn't think we were that close to the edge."

"It's possible," Kyle responded without moving his eyes from Aidan so much as an inch. "It's a grotto, and that ceiling collapsed, so it could be nothing more than our collective weight was too much for it and we were too close to the edge. It was dark, so it's hard to know."

Gunther's hands glowed with an otherworldly light as he ran them above Aidan's body. Aidan flinched and twisted, moaning. Gunther tensed with his healing effort. Guilt convulsed in my stomach at the insanity of the situation playing out before my eyes.

Aidan was a close friend in my old life, and now he lay on a rock at the bottom of a grotto I never knew existed, while my boyfriend mended his broken body. A body that wouldn't be broken if he had never met me. He lay in pain while his boyfriend looked on. A boyfriend that walked away from his old life when he suddenly discovered he was a centaur.

Again, because of me.

I was a one-woman wrecking crew.

"Stop that," Gunther said out loud through clenched teeth. The glow from his hands flared. "No one is here because they *don't* want to be here, Charlotte. Everyone made a choice, so just stop it."

"What's this about?" Kyle's eyes flashed over to me and then back to Aidan.

"Charlotte's feeling guilty," Aidan whispered and he flinched again.

"You don't even need my powers," Gunther murmured. His fingers flexed away from Aidan's body and the light glowing from his hands seemed to shift into a concentrated, brighter beam from his palm.

"I know Charlotte well," Aidan gasped as his back arched. Kyle covered his eyes with his hand for a moment and exhaled loudly. Within two beats his eyes were back on Aidan's suffering face, his own face growing as pale as his boyfriend's. "Although I will be fine in thirty seconds, that I suffered at all will make

Charlotte's insides eat themselves for at least two days."

"I think thirty seconds may be a little ambitious," Gunther said.

"The pain is lessening," Aidan told him.

"Well, thank goodness for that!" I placed a hand on Kyle's shoulder and ignored that Gunther and Aidan were talking about me. It took a lot of willpower not to argue back with them, but what was I going to say? I felt guilty, and the longer this grand adventure went on, the more guilty I felt about the consequences to my friends.

I leaned against the flat rock, my legs still beneath the water to my knees. I couldn't see what I was standing on, but I assumed the rocks on the water's edge were stacked beneath the surface. Kyle kneeled in front of me on the flat, slanted rock. He was far enough away from Aidan that Gunther could do his work but close enough he could reach out and touch Aidan if he needed to. Gunther was on the opposite side, hovering his hands above Aidan's head. I couldn't tell whether the beads of water that clung to him were from the exertion of the healing or the drenching we had taken upon falling in.

"I think that's it." Gunther leaned back. "How do you feel? Does anything still hurt?"

Aidan slowly sat up as Kyle scrambled to get closer to him. He shook his head no.

"I feel fantastic, actually. That's an amazing skill you have."

"It was my elective in witch school," Gunther shrugged. He balled his hands into fists and then flexed them outward multiple times as if the circulation in them had become sluggish. Shaking them vigorously, he then dragged his palms across his jeans and sighed. "There is nothing I hate more than the feeling of wet denim."

"Surely you have a way to remove the water," a voice called from the darkness. Aidan scrambled to his feet and our heads snapped outward. It impressed me how quickly we had shifted from the concern for Aidan to an attentive defensiveness, scanning the blackness surrounding us outside the gentle illumination of the orb.

"Can you make that any brighter?" I whispered to Gunther. He nodded and closed his eyes to concentrate.

"I *knew* you had real power. I *knew* it," Raven Goodfellow hissed from the other side of the grotto as Gunther's glowing light orb flared to full power.

The five of us stared at one another across the jade green pool. Raven stood with arms crossed, behind a moss-covered limestone slab. A hole in the grotto wall outlined him in darkness. I scanned around the entire cave quickly and realized that man-sized hole was the only one in the entire open-air cavern we had fallen into.

"I guess you can't fly," Raven said with some regret. "If you *could*, I'm sure you would be out of here by now."

"What are you doing here?" I asked him.

"What am *I* doing here? This is a holy place for witches. *Human* witches," Raven answered. He drifted toward us to the right of the entrance. "There are underwater caves leading off from this grotto that witches and slaves used for hundreds of years to hide from persecutors. Our gods have made this place for us. The warmth protects us. The fish feed us. The water nourishes us. We could live out our lives here, hidden, if we needed to."

As if to punctuate his speech, a fish jumped out of the warm water and splashed back down.

"Where is Tabitha?" I snapped at Raven accusatorially.

"If Tabitha was here, and I am *not* saying she is, but *if* she was here, it would be because *she* wishes to hide," the pale Raven shrugged. His skinny arms opened wide as he spoke. "This place is a place we come to hide. Why would I betray her and tell you? *If* she was here, mind you," Raven said with a dismissive wave of his hand. "And she's not."

Tabitha's face appeared before my eyes and a wave of dizziness crashed over me.

"How did you come here?" Raven asked, pausing his slow creep toward our side of the grotto. "How did you even *find* this place? Is it your magic? Did your magic lead you here?"

"She's here," I said out loud as my hands slowly flailed out for someone to grab onto. I superimposed Tabitha's face over the fuzzy grotto scene with great effort, like a film that had been double exposed to two images. My hand contacted someone's arm, and I held on tightly to keep from falling. "She's trying to tell me something," I said. The vision of Tabitha seemed to shout silently while her hands waved wildly.

"Listen to the image, Charlotte," Gunther's voice called from my right. He sounded faint, his voice drowned out by a freight train running over my eardrums. At least that's what it felt like, what it sounded like. "If you relax, if you concentrate..."

"I'm trying!" I shouted at him.

"Stay away from us," Kyle warned Raven. The roar in my head hurt.

"The four of you are powerful, supernatural creatures," Raven's voice echoed within the chaos of competing sights and sounds in my eyes and ears and mind. "What could I *possibly* do to creatures like you? You couldn't possibly be frightened of *me*."

"I said *stay back*," Kyle shouted. I felt movement around me as the image of Tabitha grew stronger before my eyes. It was so solid it was blocking out my ability to see what was happening in the grotto.

"Try to listen, Charlotte, listen through the noise of the energy."

"I can't do anything *but* listen! It's like the sound is being hammered right into my brain!" I gasped. The images of Tabitha and the grotto flipped, swimming before my eyes. My body swayed back and forth as the two competing realities sought to claim me. My hand, wrapped around the arm of someone near me felt, fuzzy. My fingers were dissolving, or they were on fire. I couldn't tell which anymore. I couldn't think.

"It's coming at you like a waterfall," Gunther shouted as he struggled to break through. "Don't drown in it! You can block out the images and the sound coming at you! Realize you have control, Charlotte, and *take back control*!"

Standing up under the onslaught of images and sounds and emotions made me *wish* I had lost consciousness. The roaring was deafening and… yet it didn't seem like a *sound*. It was as if it was within my brain pushing outwards, and the pressure was *incredible*. Tabitha continued to look concerned and angry, her mouth moving rapidly and her hands waving frantically as if she was desperately trying to get across a message I couldn't understand.

"I can't hear you! I don't understand what you're trying to tell me!" I shouted at Tabitha.

"Charlotte, relax and focus on *hearing her voice*!"

"All I can hear is the roaring! It's like a tornado, like a freight train, and it's getting louder and louder! I can't hear you, Tabitha! Where are you?" I gasped and felt every muscle in my body twang with tension. The images flashed before my eyes, and my brain, wrapping around me like a rope, pushing out from within me...I wanted it to stop, I wanted it all to stop, but I fought to keep from pushing it away. I had to get to Tabitha. I had to know what was happening.

It felt like the roar would break me apart. The sound and feeling and pounding grew louder and harder and...

I felt my legs buckle as I crumpled, sliding off the rock and into the deep water.

# CHAPTER 11

As soon as my head slipped beneath the surface of the water the roaring in my ears... stopped.

It was as if the water acted as a protector, controlling the images and sounds that had been coming at me. They felt muffled. Though I could still see Tabitha in my mind's eye, the pressure within my head was gone. The roaring that had been so loud I thought my eardrums would burst was now a low murmur.

"Charlotte, can you hear me?" Tabitha's faint voice reached me in whispered tendrils.

The water was warm, so warm. My feet hit the bottom of the grotto's pool and I felt the panic rise within me. That connection with the bottom of the flooded cavern, though, was the only way I had to orient myself. Swiveling my head around, the water was difficult to see through. Above me, there *could* be an ill-defined light but I wasn't sure. I bent my legs and kicked off the bottom, heading toward what I *believed* was the top.

As I hit a rock with force, I heard a muffled clunk. I felt as if my lungs would burst as my hands probed along the flat boulder. Surely this was up. It *had* to be.

Didn't it?

*Relax, Charlotte, you can't drown, remember? Just let out your breath. Then breathe in the water if it makes you more comfortable. Whether you do or not, you'll be fine.*

My lungs were on fire. It was a familiar feeling, one I knew from childhood. That feeling we would make ourselves have by diving too far down in the deep end of the pool. Contests at the local Y to see which one of us could hold our breath and touch the grate at the bottom. I knew what this felt like. I knew what this was. My chest burned.

Gunther was wrong, I would drown here.

*You will not, Charlotte. I would never let anything happen to you. I promise you. You can't drown.*

As I tried to get control of my rising panic, I realized that I wasn't getting dizzy. I wasn't seeing stars or feeling like I would pass out. It was just a burning in my lungs as I struggled not to exhale. I held my breath for far too long, and the $CO_2$ was building. That's why it burns. I knew that from school.

It hurt so badly. My body screaming its warning for me to find air.

If it hurt this bad, didn't it mean *I could drown?*

*No, Charlotte, just let out your breath. I promise you, you'll be fine.*

I wanted to trust Gunther, but it was too crazy an idea. It was so wrong, so against the instinct I had that I couldn't do it. I couldn't release the last bit of air I had without knowing where the next gulp would come from. I didn't know where the surface was. I moaned as my hands desperately clawed against the rock looking for an air pocket, anything—

*Charlotte. Trust me.*

No.

"Charlotte! Charlotte, can you hear me?" Tabitha called, and what had been a whisper was now strong. It sounded closer, clear.

"Tabitha?" I called, the breath I had been holding exploding out of my mouth in a torrent of bubbles and gurgling. Without thinking, I inhaled the water sharply, panicked it would fill my lungs and I would never see the light of day again. My chest ached with the effort, but the pain I felt from holding my last breath of real air didn't return.

*I told you.*

*I don't understand how I'm doing this,* I thought to Gunther with wonder. All the magic things I had seen since I became ringmaster, all the things I had done, all the power I had…For some reason, *this* dazzled me more than any of it. I was beneath the surface of the water, down below where the fish lived. Deep underneath in the darkness.

And I was fine.

It was amazing.

*The magic protects you from many situations. I don't know precisely how you're doing it, either, I just know this is how witches survived the medieval tests. Sure, we would sink but somehow we could extract enough oxygen out of the water even though we shouldn't be able to. Maybe the magic makes more oxygen, maybe it calls it to you. I don't know. I just know you'll be fine.*

"Tabitha, can you hear me?" I said again. Despite being capable of existing underwater and extracting oxygen from the warm liquid, my ability to talk did *not* improve in any capacity. My voice left my lips in a gurgling symphony of bubbling word-like sounds. I could see an image of her faintly in the water.

"Charlotte, are you underwater? Just nod if you can hear me, I can see you!"

I nodded yes. Tabitha clapped her hands together and smiled when I answered her.

"Are you at Magician's Pool? Well, I guess you would be *in* Magician's Pool, if we want to get technical about it." Tabitha motioned to what I assumed was an image of me in front of her, wet. I held my hands up and shrugged with some exaggeration to make it clear to her I had no idea where I was. "Is it the big grotto near where I left my car?" I nodded yes.

"I'm here, Charlotte! I'm in one of the chambers off the pool!"

I didn't remember seeing any chambers off the pool. The only hole I had seen after we fell in the water was the carved doorway behind Raven Goodfellow. I assumed that led in and out of the cavern. Just the thought of that stupid gothic idiot was enough to light my anger anew. He must've kidnapped Tabitha. But why?

*If he did, I think I know why,* Gunther said. A bright white light appeared ten feet to my left at about twenty feet up. *That should help you get to the surface. I think you should hear this.*

*You could have just helped me get to the top whenever, but instead you left me down here flailing?* I thought as I swam toward the light.

*I wouldn't put it like that, but look at the new skill you just picked up,* Gunther pointed out. *And if you think that I am unaware of how amazing you just found the experience, think again, my love.*

You and I will have words about this.

*Probably not right now,* Gunther said. *All hell has broken loose up here.*

As my head broke the surface, I spotted skinny Raven Goodfellow running on his spindly legs around the outskirts of the grotto pool. Kyle raced after him, his powerful legs launching him over rocks and boulders as if he were an Olympic gold medal track star. Whatever arrogance Raven had displayed at the start of our confrontation, it was *gone* now.

"Come back here, you arrogant little snot!" Kyle bellowed. His boots thundered against the limestone rocks. Raven squealed like a field mouse being chased by a panther. "If you want to make threats and call people names, you better be able to *back them up!*"

"*What* threats?" I asked, pulling myself out of the water and onto one of the rocks.

"Raven over here told Kyle that he was going to have all of our powers, and that once he had all of our powers he was going to beat Kyle up," Gunther told me from two rocks away. He glanced at the two men as they raced, and flashed a worried expression. "He said it with a lot more bluff and bluster—and also insulted Kyle and Aidan's relationship in some rather, ah…vulgar terms. It didn't sit very well with Kyle."

"What did he mean, he'd have all of our powers?" I asked Gunther, confused.

"I guess we'll have to ask him that once Kyle catches him," Gunther responded.

"He won't be in any shape to answer any questions once I catch him!" Kyle snarled. Raven shrieked when the centaur elegantly sailed over the moss covered rocks toward his prey.

"This isn't exactly hell breaking loose," I said, crossing my arms. "And it doesn't look like Raven can say anything at all. The kid is panting so hard he looks like a human bellows."

"It might be once Kyle catches him," Aidan said. We slowly picked our way over to Aidan's limestone slab and sat down next to him. The grotto was so large that the circumference around the pool might be a quarter of a mile to run. "I've only seen him look like that when he was on the force chasing bad guys."

"Kyle, we have to question him!" I hollered. Despite the size of the grotto, my voice echoed and carried everywhere. "We can't question him while he's running full speed away from you!"

"Tell her what she wants to know!" Kyle barked at the twenty-something who was scrambling over a rock. "For every answer you give her that's helpful to us, I'll slow down a little bit. *Maybe.*"

"That's ridiculous!" Raven squealed. He glanced back behind him and careened off the rock wall. It was clear that Raven Goodfellow's physical prowess was not enough that he could keep up his get-away attempt for long. He also didn't seem to have counted on the grotto being a circle, and the four-foot path around the circumference of the pool gave him no alternative escape routes.

He was on the other side of the pool from us now, but the circle pathway had only two directions to get to the *one* cut-out doorway in the natural room. He had to go through us, or go through Kyle.

That simple fact hadn't seemed to dawn on him yet.

"That's the deal! Charlotte, ask him!" Kyle shouted, his voice echoing back. The centaur slowed down to a leisurely jog. Raven was so panicked that he didn't even notice the gift of distance Kyle had given him.

"*Where* is Tabitha, Raven?" I demanded. Her image flickered in front of my eyes and then faded.

"I told you she's not here!"

"Oh, goody, I get to beat him to a pulp," Kyle said excitedly and launched himself over a boulder. Raven's eyes grew wide and panicked.

"In the ritual room! She's in the ritual room!" he shrieked, red splotches starting to take over his pale complexion. "It's under the water now! She'll come out when the water goes down! No one did anything to her!"

"What do you mean she's *under* the water?" I scanned the still, murky depths between us. "How can she be under the water?"

"Because you can normally get to the ritual room! She got to the ritual room! And then it rained and the pool filled up. She's not under the water, *the room* is under the water," he explained in a high-pitched voice and dramatically launched himself over a relatively small limestone slab. With a tumble and a thump, he slammed against the rock wall. Kyle rolled his eyes, casually jogging behind Raven.

"Why didn't you just tell the police that? She's been stuck in a dark cave underwater *all this time?*" I shuddered.

"No one knows about this place, and *no one will,*" Raven said harshly. He stopped running. Kyle paused behind him. "There's food, fresh water, and bedding in there. We are not *idiots*, you know. It's happened before. In fact, initiates have to spend the night within the earth before joining the coven after the rains. We *all* do it."

I walked over to the dark oval hole in the side of the grotto wall and looked down at the path floor. There were stone steps carved from fallen boulders leading straight into the water. In the darkness, they disappeared. Looking up, I could see that the collapsed dome was softer in some places. Water dripped from those sections, and then I understood.

"It must be an underwater cavern," I called to Gunther and Aidan. "When it's dry, it's exposed and you can walk right in. That's probably most of the time in this part of Texas. Once it rains here, though, all sorts of things can flood." I turned back and glared. "Why not at least tell her parents where she is, Raven? They *are* members of your coven. They know about this place, don't they?"

"My master knows *exactly* where the child is," Raven snapped and then slammed his two hands over his mouth. His eyes careened as he took in our shocked faces. Removing his hands, he stammered. "We've *all* spent a day or three in the cavern after a flood, so her parents knew she was fine." Kyle took a loud step behind him and the goth shrieked. He scrambled toward us again.

It was possible that Raven spoke to them after Aidan and I had visited, but something about his explanation…

"What did you mean? That you were going to have all of our powers?" I asked him.

"I don't know *what* you're talking about," Raven said as he ran toward us. The son of the high priestess suddenly put two and two together. His face was a mess of frustration and anger when he realized he was headed straight toward us. He looked toward the pool, and then back behind him to see if Kyle was still there.

He was.

"Dude, it's a big *circle*," I told him. His face paled beneath the red splotches. "There's nowhere for you to go. We are standing in front of the only door in or out of this place. Just calm down and *talk* to us."

"No!" He shouted and jumped into the water. Awkwardly doggy paddling away from us and Kyle, he turned around and trod water. "I just have to stay away from you until your powers are mine! I was promised! I was promised I could be a real paranormal!"

"We are not paranormals!" I protested.

"You're a liar!" He spat at me and moved further toward the center of the pool. "Tabitha figured out what you were. We *know*. We know about the power and how it passes, we know about the circus. We know *all about you*. We study and work *for years* to understand magic, and you just stumble through it like idiots. You *don't* deserve it. We *deserve* it and we're going to *take* it from you."

He knows all about us. Was there anyone left in this town that didn't?

"Raven, it doesn't work like that," I told him. I stood on the edge of the water looking down. "It's not like it is in books or movies where someone bites you and you become a werewolf, or vampire bites you and you become a vampire."

"That actually does work like that. The vampire thing, I mean," Gunther told me.

"Oh. Well, other than the vampire thing, being a paranormal doesn't work like that," I told the soggy human witch. "It's just who we are, Raven. You can't take my powers. My powers have to do with my bloodline and my family. I couldn't give them to you if I wanted to. I am who I am, and you are who you are."

"Do we really think it's a good idea to admit to this moron what we are?" Kyle asked.

I shrugged. "I feel like everyone seems to know who we are at this point."

"You're an idiot," Raven shouted. "None of you know the first thing about what *you* are, what you can do. My master and I have studied and worked for years to learn about power and how to wield it. We are on the cusp of achieving what we sought."

My eyes narrowed. "What are you talking about?"

"Like I said, you're an idiot," Raven said ominously, a tight smile on his lips. "You don't even realize the power *your own blood* holds. How someone with access to it could examine it, figure out what makes it special, and use it to take what you never should've had in the first place."

"Charlotte—" Kyle said.

"Darius Stevens," Aidan said, jumping up. "The tech company that he works for? It's a biomedical research company. You and I used to donate blood all the time, Charlotte. It's conceivable that—"

"He has my blood," I muttered. I could practically feel my brain snapping pieces into place.

"I just needed to keep you and Tabitha out of the way," Raven said proudly. We all turned to stare at him and his arrogance wilted as he shuddered under our intense scrutiny. "Look, no one got hurt! It's not right that you all have so much power and we work so hard for almost none! It's not fair! We are just trying to even the playing field! Get what we deserve! We're tired of being kicked all the time!"

"I'll give you what you deserve," Kyle muttered and stomped over the fallen limestone slabs toward Raven. The bobbing human witch shrieked in panic and frantically pushed himself in the opposite direction.

"Did you lead Tabitha here on purpose?" I asked Raven.

"My master needed her safely out of the way," Raven told me. "No one was hurt."

"Why did he need her out of the way?"

"So she wouldn't be hurt when we went to take the power," Raven explained. "We didn't want her to figure out what was happening. We didn't want her to try and stop us. She would, too. She's always been too smart for her own good, and she would never let us finish."

"Why not?" I asked him, confused about why Tabitha would side against her own family.

Raven blinked. "Well, in case stealing your power killed you, of course."

"This whole thing was a set-up," I told Aidan, Gunther and Kyle quietly. We were gathered on the edge of the grotto pool. "I think Darius Stevens planned this whole thing. He had Raven bring Tabitha down here right before a hard rain. He knew as soon as I found out she was missing I would come back here. Her disappearance was just to lure the Magical Midway back to Mickwac."

"Can he really steal Charlotte's power?" Kyle asked glancing back at Raven.

"That idiot? No," Aidan said. "But Darius? He seemed awfully confident when we met at his house. He's really smart. And there have been some times in history that humans have been able to get paranormal power by force."

"I thought the whole point of the Magical Midway and the circuses and what Maggie did was to remove their ability to do that? Don't you need magic to get magic?" I asked him.

"Maybe nobody is quite as powerful as they think they are, including Maggie," Kyle shrugged. "Tabitha's been able to reach out to you off and on since you got here. That indicates she has *some* type of magical power. Doesn't it? Humans are more creative than the Witches' Council gives them credit for."

"I'm not going to be any help here," Gunther said. "I went all the way in witch school and they were pretty insistent that the humans had exactly zero magical power on their own. According to the Witches' Council, paranormals are the source of all magic in the world."

"Well, clearly *that's* not the case," I told him quickly. "If we assume that it's possible Darius and Raven have the capability of doing whatever it is they *think* they're going to do, we have a problem. And I think we have to assume that they could. If we assume the Witches' Council is right and they can't, we're going to be awfully surprised if they do."

"If they do what, exactly?" Kyle asked.

"That's just it. We still don't know," I told him.

"We have to know what they know, at least as much as we can," Gunther said.

"Agreed. I need to swim down and see if I can get Tabitha out," I told them. Claws of fear scratched at my insides. Intellectually, I understood that I couldn't drown. Emotionally, however, I would rather throw myself full force at the limestone wall ten times in a row until the clanging rattled my brain than swim back down into that inky blackness.

"I'll come with you, Charlotte," Gunther said. Kyle and Aidan nodded. I was grateful that if I had to go into the darkness and breathe liquid again that I wouldn't have to do it alone.

"I think Kyle and I need to go back to the Magical Midway," Aidan said, a tight smile on his lips. "I hate to leave you here, and even more so without a vehicle. But we need to warn your uncle and the lares guards. We don't know *what* they're planning, but it sounds like they have to be on the fairgrounds to try whatever it is they intend to try."

"Agreed. What we do about him?" I hitched my thumb in Raven's direction.

"I'm just fine where I am, thanks!" Raven called.

"Nothing. Though stealing his car might not be a bad idea," Gunther grinned that familiar and mischievous smile.

"You are *not taking* my Mazda Miata!" Raven screamed. He flailed around in the water in protest.

"That settles it," I said turning to Aidan. "You two take his Miata, it's a two-seater. Gunther and I will need a back seat for Tabitha."

"You can't just leave me here!"

"The way you left Tabitha? *For days?*" I snapped as I eyed him. "We sure can, and we sure *will.*"

"Go," Gunther said. "We may not have much time."

"Don't we need the keys for his car?" Aidan asked.

"*Please.*" Kyle rolled his eyes. "Keys. What kind of ex-cop do you take me for?"

Aidan nodded. I watched the two of them as they made their way over to the dark oval exit. Then they disappeared. Gunther and I were left in the grotto with a relieved Raven Goodfellow still treading water in the center of the pool. He made no move in any direction.

"Let's go get your friend, shall we?" Gunther held out his hand and I took it. "Considering how many times she's tried to project herself directly into your mind, I suspect she'll be pretty happy to see you."

# CHAPTER 12

"WE KNOW THAT IT'S IN *THAT* GENERAL DIRECTION," Gunther pointed to the right. We slid our legs into the water. "I have a spell that should be able to guide me on the path, but you won't be able to see it."

"What you want me to do?" I asked him as we clung to the slabs in the water. The warmth was now up to my chin, and I felt Gunther's hand reach for mine somewhere beneath the surface. Raven Goodfellow watched us quietly from the other side of the pool.

"Just don't let go of me, Charlotte." He smiled, his eyes softening as he gazed at me. "That's all I ever want."

I blushed.

"Oh, ew," Raven said. He followed it with a retching sound. We ignored him.

"Are you ready?" Gunther asked, his face morphing from mushy adoration to steely concentration. "If you have any problems, just think them to me. I'll have to concentrate on the spell to get us there as quickly as possible, but I'll hear you, and I will do whatever I can to help if you need it."

I nodded, and our heads sank below the water into the murky green darkness.

My chest burned again almost instantly. I struggled to will myself to give up the air within my lungs. Even though I had done this before, and I accepted that I wouldn't drown and die in this cave, the instinct for self-preservation wasn't an easy one to let go of. My face felt searingly hot, hotter than the abnormally warm water that surrounded us.

*You have to just let it go, Charlotte. Your tension and paranoia are causing half of your problem.*

Tension and paranoia had kept me safe. I couldn't let it go.

The discomfort wasn't enough for me to release that air. I grimaced as my feet left the rocks collected on the side of the pool and darkness closed in. The light from above had gone out when Gunther's focus shifted to the path below. The water was now a warm, rayless emptiness. Gunther pulled me along a path that only he saw as we swam toward Tabitha.

It might have been peaceful if I wasn't terrified of the slimy, feathery touches that brushed my face.

*Just fish, Charlotte,* Gunther thought soothingly. His hand around mine squeezed. *We are in a freshwater pool, and there are fish here. They are not nearly as afraid of you as you are of them,* he told me.

I *knew* all that. I mean, Gunther was thinking the obvious. I knew there were fish in a freshwater pool, for goodness sake. It didn't mean I wanted them tapping my skin in greeting. I jumped again when something brushed my nose.

The stinging in my chest built into a crescendo of demand that I get the heck out of here and *breathe*. My left hand flailed into the wet emptiness looking for support, the surface, a rock…Anything, I didn't care. Suddenly, Gunther yanked me hard toward him and our bodies slammed against one another.

*You're going to hate me for this and I am really, really sorry, but—*

Gunther didn't even finish the thought before

he placed his palm on my diaphragm and pushed. Hard. Gurgles of air bubbles and protest exploded through my mouth and I pushed him away frantically.

*Charlotte, don't push me, I'll lose you in the darkness—*

His observation came just a moment too late. His hand slipped from mine. I stretched my hand frantically in the last direction I remembered Gunther being, but it connected with nothing. I kicked my feet frantically trying to find the pool floor or a slab to hold on to, but I found nothing. I was alone in the darkness. I couldn't tell which way was up or down, left or right.

Well, left or right, okay. I *knew* which was my left and which was my right.

Not that it *helped* me while I floated in the all-encompassing blackness.

*Don't move, I'll find you.*

*Why can't I ever find you?* I thought back to him angrily. *I am so tired of feeling like some weak-willed damsel in distress around you.* I could feel him recoil in shock from my thought.

I felt bad for thinking it. But I couldn't help it. Ever since he showed up with his super-magic and his advanced ringmaster tricks, I was feeling like a complete embarrassment. I lost track of how often Gunther had to rescue me, said something smarter than me, came up with a better idea than me.

I didn't like it.

I was not used to feeling like someone who needed rescue. I had never done it in my human life, never dated those men that liked their women to be wilting flowers with a coquettish laugh and a submissive head tilt. I hated that Gunther so consistently made me feel like a failure. He didn't *mean* to. He just did, by being who he was.

*If I were one of your human medical doctors, would you feel inferior because you couldn't do open heart surgery and I could?* Gunther asked me as I felt his hands close around my shoulders.

*That's completely different, that's a matter of education and training,* I told him.

*So is this,* Gunther thought as he wrapped his arms around me and held me in the warm water.

*We are both witches,* I disagreed. *And now we're both ringmasters.*

*Yes, but only one of us is trained. We start as youngsters, Charlotte, and we train for years on how to best use our powers, how to find and cultivate our particular talents,* Gunther thought and his hand ran through my floating hair. *Even with my late start, I am years ahead of you. You wouldn't fault yourself for not knowing something you never had the chance to learn in the human world. Don't do it here.*

*I just hate that you're better than me,* I grumbled.

*I'm not better than you, Charlotte,* Gunther thought, hugging me. *Both of our talents, our training, our abilities and our way of looking at the world have been needed at different times since I met you. I'm not better than you. Just different. One thing I am sure of, though. You and I are both better together.*

I blushed, happy that he couldn't see.

Gunther was always so calm, so steady. But the thing I most loved about him was his ability to re-frame my own failures and my self-consciousness into something positive. I doubted myself and yet with Gunther in my head? I hadn't been able to doubt myself for long on *anything.* He was always there to tell me that things were not as dire as I thought they were.

Well, not as much lately, since he moved back to the Makepeace Circus—

I felt a stab of pain in Gunther, but before I could ask him about it, it was gone.

*We are close to the entrance of the cave,* Gunther said. He pulled away and slid his hand down my arm to thread his fingers through mine again. It felt as if he was squeezing just a little bit more tightly. *Are you ready to see her?*

I nodded, and somehow he knew.

"Charlotte!" Tabitha shouted as we emerged from the slanted underwater pathway into the ritual room. "I can't believe you found me!"

Tabitha, who had always been dressed neatly, was covered in dank, wet mud. It clung to her clothing and was smudged on her arms. A clump of it gathered in her blond hair. "You look absolutely awful," I told my friend and made my way across the small room with open arms. "I was so worried about you."

"*You* were worried about *me?*" She pulled back, her big blue eyes wide. "I thought you were kidnapped by demons and roasting over the fires of hell! Or something equally terrible! Charlotte, how could you not tell me where you were going and what had happened to you?"

My pulse raced.

Since we had arrived back in Mickwac, it had become clear there were more people that knew of our existence than there should be. People that shouldn't know. Humans that should never be able to find out because they weren't hidden paranormals. I mean, I had never really spoken to a human that knew of us who wasn't exposed as a hidden paranormal in almost the *very* next second.

Aidan found out as the Magical Midway was claiming him as a paranormal. His discovery of what I was coincided with his discovery of what *he* was, and so it wasn't strange for him. Well, it wasn't any *more* strange discovering me, anyway. The same thing happened with Kyle.

But this was someone I had been friends with, close friends with, for years. And Tabitha had visited the Magical Midway with me years ago, so I *knew* she wasn't a hidden paranormal.

Fear was blossoming within my gut again, eclipsing the excitement I had felt just moments before at seeing Tabitha Stevens alive. I just got her out of danger. How much danger would reconnecting with me put her back *in*?

"I wasn't really allowed to tell anybody where I was going, Tabitha," I told her, my eyes gazing distractedly at the accoutrements decorating the submerged room. Candles flickered from tiny recesses in the walls, and a bed roll was unfurled against the far wall behind what looked like an altar. "What have you been doing down here?"

Tabitha tilted her chin higher and raised her eyebrow. "Really? You want to know what I've been *doing* down here?"

"I just...I mean...It seemed like a legitimate question," I told her. I walked to my right and examined a doll sitting on a rock. My mind twisted into pretzels trying to figure out what to say to Tabitha now that she was in front of me. I couldn't talk about where I'd been. It wasn't safe to talk about what *she* knew.

Just five minutes ago this meeting seemed like it would be easy.

Now, I didn't know what to do, how to put the distance back between us that had to exist. So I talked about the weather.

"Why would you come down here on a day it was forecast to rain?" I asked her casually.

"Are you really not going to admit that you're a *real* witch?" Tabitha crossed her arms. "After *lying* to me about you and Aidan dating, after *lying* to me about your relationship, after treating me like someone you couldn't confide in or be *honest* with," Tabitha said sharply. She pulled her shoulders back and her eyes narrowed. "You mean to tell me you'd rather check out the doll in an underwater ritual room off of the pool that no one but occult practitioners even knows exists rather than be honest with me? *Still?*"

"Hey, I apologized to you about the Aidan thing—"

"Did you *really* think an apology was going to make up for the fact that every time the four of us were together, you were putting on a show for me?" Tabitha stepped toward me and shook her finger in my direction. "I had a right to be angry at you!"

"I never said you didn't," I frowned, raising my voice and stepping back.

"You disappeared before I even had time to work through any forgiveness I might've found!"

"It couldn't be helped—"

"I know that! Don't you think I *know that*?" Tabitha shouted angrily, her voice echoing off the walls of rock. "I know all about you, *Ringmaster.* I know who you are, I know what the Magical Midway is, I know about all of it, Charlotte."

"I'm not sure what you think you know—" I began, frightened by her words.

"Don't you dare," she whispered. Her eyes filled with tears and her fists balled so tightly her knuckles turned white. "Don't you dare pretend what I said wasn't true. Don't you dare lie to me again. Don't you dare act like you're not here because I projected my spirit into your stupid brain!"

"Like I'm not…wait, what? Okay, you know what? *Fine*," I snapped at Tabitha, my own anger bubbling up out of the pool of fear that had knotted up my stomach since I came back to Mickwac. "How did you keep your home life from me *all those years*? Never once, not *once* did you ever tell me that your mother was an alcoholic or your father was a workaholic, or they were both witches. Not once!"

"They are *not* witches, they're just human—"

"Wait a minute, you *had* your say—"

"I don't know *what* you think you know, Charlotte, but I—"

"What I *think* I know? What I *think* I know? I *saw* your dysfunctional parents—"

Gunther leaned wearily against the rock wall watching the two of us as we faced each other down. Tabitha heard absolutely nothing I said, and I heard nothing she said. Despite that, we were like two kettles venting built-up steam that time, distance, and anger had trapped. After five minutes of cutting each other off with such deft precision that not *one single full thought* had been communicated, both of us stopped, and panted, and stared daggers at one another.

"Are you both done?" Gunther asked quietly from his perch. We glared at him.

"It's clear that you both had to keep secrets from one another. Whatever your motivation, I certainly don't see that either one of you intended to hurt the other." Gunther pushed himself off the wall. "Charlotte, you raced back here to find your friend even though you didn't know if she would ever talk to you again. Tabitha, out of all the people that you could have reached out to, your tie to Charlotte was the one that you utilized for rescue. I realize you're both angry and hurt about the actions of the other, but it seems to me you have both equally hidden yourselves, and you also both equally care. It's a level playing field to start. If you can stop shouting at one another long enough, that is, to see that."

Dripping water echoed in the silence and Gunther's words doused the fires of our anger. Tabitha wrapped her arms around herself as she watched me. Then she nodded to no one in particular.

"Look, I didn't reach out to Charlotte because I cared about her," Tabitha disagreed with Gunther, who raised his eyebrow. "Well, yes, okay, I did…I *do* care about her, I'm not saying I don't. But I was trying to connect with her soul to soul to warn her about Raven and my father. I could've stayed down here for weeks," she said, waving her hands around the small ritual room. "I'm glad I don't have to, but I *could* have."

"What you mean, warn me about your father?"

"Charlotte, I am so sorry." Tabitha grabbed my arm. "My father found out all of the information I was able to put together. He lured you here because he believes he can steal your power."

"He can't, though." I told her. "Right? He can't do that."

Gunther's forehead wrinkled with concern. After a few moments, he answered. "With what we've always believed? No. But a lot of things have been happening because of this prophecy that have greatly changed things that we always believed. I wouldn't assume that he can't."

"Oh, right, the thirteenth witch prophecy thing," Tabitha nodded. I turned to her, shocked.

"You know about the prophecy?"

"Of course," Tabitha nodded. "I mean, it's our fault, isn't it?"

I nodded. "Wait, what?" I asked her, confused.

"The prophecy can wait," Gunther said. "We need to get back to the Magical Midway, and we need to get Tabitha out of this wet prison cell."

"Oh, it hasn't been so bad," Tabitha shrugged.

"I should have known when Raven suggested that we come to the ritual room without the rest of the coven that something was up. He said he wanted to meditate. He doesn't *really* meditate."

"He claims that your father knows you're here," I told her as we walked to the water's edge.

"Of course he does." Tabitha shuddered. "Dad needed to get you here somehow. There's something on the Magical Midway grounds that he believes will help him steal your power. He had to get you here to take it."

"How do you know that?"

"Raven told me," Tabitha responded. "Once he had me stuck down here, I guess there was no reason to hide anything anymore."

"Do you know what it is? This thing they're going to steal?" She shook her head no.

"I'm sure Kyle and Aidan can handle it, but I still think we need to get back there with all due haste," Gunther said, and then his hands began moving in a rhythmic pattern around Tabitha's head.

Tabitha was dazzled by the magical dome that Gunther created from the neck up so she could breathe while he pulled both of us back to the surface. Her eyes were as wide as I had ever seen them when he popped the encasement once we reached the rocks.

"There won't be any residual effects," he said.

"Where's Raven?" I asked, looking around.

"Raven was here?" Tabitha asked with some surprise.

"We left him treading water on that side of the grotto," Gunther told her. "I imagine he decided to take his leave of this place while we were in the ritual room with you."

"Thank you…Um, I'm sorry, I don't know your name," Tabitha said with a smile. She pulled herself up the slanted rock and walked toward the path briskly. "Are you one of Charlotte's friends from the Magical Midway?"

"More than friends," I told her. We made our way to the exit. "This is Gunther Makepeace. He's the ringmaster of the Makepeace Circus, and my boyfriend."

"So you're a witch too, then?" Tabitha asked with amusement woven through her words. I glanced up and rolled my eyes when she looked back with a barely suppressed grin.

"I am, yes," Gunther said.

"Well, that's probably good. You'll need magic powers to date Charlotte," Tabitha joked.

"Here we go," I rolled my eyes again and looked down.

"I'm not saying that she's challenging to date," Tabitha laughed, gesturing toward me. "I'm just saying the longest romantic relationship I ever saw her have with a man was the one she had with Aidan, and he was gay."

"But I knew he was gay," I pointed out.

"That kinda makes it worse, Charlotte," Tabitha snorted. "When they were straight you'd usually chase them off within a date or two."

"Okay, again, that's not *really* fair." I entered the darkened rock hallway, my feet on the steps leading out of the grotto. "I could see what they were thinking when they were on a date with me. That was really never conducive to making me want a second date with anybody."

"Speaking of that," Tabitha asked from behind me. "You're telepathic, right?"

For a moment, the old familiar defenses kicked in and I almost lied. It was disconcerting how the instinct to dishonesty was the first thing I felt whenever I was questioned by humans about *anything*. The Witches' Council and its rules had created a divide between paranormals and humans that made any connection one that risked the death penalty. It was no surprise that humans were so desperate for any connection with magic and magical creatures.

I decided to simply tell the truth. It's not like the Witches' Council didn't want me dead, anyway, and Tabitha had already made it clear to anyone who was paying attention that she believed we existed.

"Sort of. There are different levels of telepathy and empathy. Mine is really strong, but it only works on one person at a time. I have to really concentrate to read someone or they have to be projecting really strongly for it to intrude on my own thoughts."

"How did you not know that Bobby was such a jerk?" Tabitha asked.

She tried to keep her voice even, but I could hear the pain along the edges of her question. When the situation between Aidan and me had come to light, it had destroyed everyone's relationship. Bobby, Aidan's best friend from high school, did not know Aidan was gay and did not react well to finding out. Tabitha, who was engaged to Bobby, was suddenly smacked in the face with the fact that her husband-to-be was an intolerant, judgmental jerk. She left him.

But she left Aidan and me, as well. Because we lied to her.

"First, in my human life? I *didn't* run around rummaging through people's heads willy-nilly," I told her. We climbed out of the dark hallway and into the cool, dry night air. After the humidity of the grotto, the soft breeze was refreshing. "I tried to maintain some sense of ethics and not push in where I wasn't invited. And since no one knew what I could do, I was never invited."

"But you could see what people were thinking when they were on a date with you," she responded, her observation tinged with a tiny bit of accusation. Gunther listened to our conversation intently, but he stayed out of the discussion.

"They were on a date with me, so they were concentrating on me," I explained. The three of us made our way down the path toward the road. "A lot of what I picked up they broadcast straight at me. Sometimes I did go in and look for their motivations just because I didn't want to invest a lot of time in a relationship with someone that was hiding—"

"Secrets?"

"*Everyone* has secrets, Tabby," I responded with my old nickname for her. "I knew I would find secrets buried in people's heads. I was more concerned with their motivation. I wanted to find someone who was truly interested in me for me. Apparently, that's not real common on a first date."

"But still, you never sensed that Bobby would have a reaction like that?"

"Maybe I didn't want to."

Tabitha stopped walking and turned to face me. "What do you mean?"

"Bobby was your fiancé *and* Aidan's best friend. Even if I *did* know he was a jerk, what was I supposed to say? How was I supposed to explain it?" I asked her. "I couldn't tell you how I knew even if I did find anything specific I could point to." Recognition dawned on her face and she nodded slightly. "You already knew I didn't like him, though, Tabby. I mean, I called him Lexus Bobby behind his back, for goodness sake. You knew I wasn't a huge fan of the guy."

"And sometimes to his face. Man, he *hated* that. Anyway…I don't know…Yeah, I guess so," she sighed. "I guess I knew you didn't like him. Boy, we really do a bang-up job of seeing what we want to see sometimes." I felt her attention change, becoming laser-focused on Gunther. A determination took hold within her. "I promise if

I think your boyfriend is a jerk, Charlotte? I'll tell you straight out."

"Thanks, I appreciate that," I nodded.

"Should I be concerned?" Gunther asked as we reached the road. It was still quiet, and the animal shelter truck was parked where we left it across the bridge.

"Not if you're not a jerk." Tabitha gave Gunther the once-over and made her way across the road.

# CHAPTER 13

"So, like, what's the dealio, boss?" Bob, the self-improvement hippie surfer lares guard, met us in front of my parents' house. It was unusual for the lares to be off the Magical Midway grounds for any reason, much less during a situation of high safety concern.

"Why are you out here?" I asked Bob.

"So, like, Kyle and Aidan were all concerned for, like, your parents' house? Since there's just a big field behind the Magical Midway they figured the humans wouldn't fly in or anything," Bob said, his spear leaning casually against his shoulder while he waved his hands animatedly in the air. "The humans all need, like, cars and trucks and motorcycles to move around? That means they have to come in on the road. And that means *right* there." Bob pointed to the driveway into the property.

"Do we really think your father would just drive up?" I asked Tabitha.

"We have a Jeep, so he could off-road in through the back without much of a problem," Tabitha said. Her eyes scanned the area around the Magical Midway. "It's pretty empty out here. I doubt anyone would notice a Jeep tootling through their back forty, you know?"

"Tootling?" Bob asked, his eyes wide. "What magic is this? What is this tootling you speak of?"

"You know, messing around, wandering in the back of the field," Tabitha said with a toss of her head. "You know, *tootling.*"

"Fascinating," Bob whispered, his eyes shining as he stared at Tabitha.

"You can also go tooling through the back forty," she said glancing back and forth between me and the unnaturally exuberant Bob. "Means basically the same thing. Go around without a direction or goal, to drive or jaunt about."

"Just by removing the T, the word has a completely different feeling," Bob exclaimed excitedly, leaning forward. "Tootle feels fun and light and airy, while tool feels heavy and important and dark," Bob told her energetically. He paused, waiting for Tabitha's reaction.

"Um. I guess so?" Her mouth twitched with a half smile. "What *are* you?"

"I am a *Bob*," he said proudly. He extended his arm outward with his palm down almost touching Tabitha's nose. She stared at him in shock.

"You have a Nazi as a guard?" Tabitha asked me.

"What? A what now?" Gunther asked.

"That's a Roman salute, Tabitha," I told her, reaching out for Bob's wrist and lowering his arm. "Bob is a lares. They were guardians in ancient Rome—

"Holy crap, you're a paranormal creature," Tabitha whispered. "Lares were deities, guardian deities, in Rome. Ancient Rome was, like, thousands of years ago. How *old* are you?"

"Old enough to know better, young enough to get away with it," Bob smarmed. He deepened his voice and waggled his eyebrows at Tabitha. He leaned into her space, but she simply stared back at him not moving.

"Are you a god?" she whispered.

"Well, now, little lady, wouldn't you prefer to find out on your own? You don't want me to spoil all your fun, do you?" he said, wrapping his arm around her shoulder.

"When I found the books, I knew what they said about what you were, Charlotte—"

"You do realize *I'm* a paranormal creature, too," I studied her mesmerized expression. "When you saw *me* for the first time after you knew, you *yelled* at me."

"Oh, stick a sock in it, Charlotte," Tabitha retorted, never taking her attention from Bob.

I stared at Gunther and held up my hands.

*Do you think we'll still get attacked if you take a human into the Magical Midway?* Gunther thought. *I may not have your telepathy, love, but the expression on Bob's face tells me that he's smitten with your human friend.*

*Maybe you and I can turn her into a magical creature,* I thought back with aggravation. *I bet she'd love to be a goblin.*

Gunther laughed out loud.

We tore Tabitha away from Bob, but it was not without effort. While we walked to the house, she kept glancing over her shoulder at the lares. He stared at her until we walked onto the porch.

Well, Bob was better than Bobby, anyway.

"Tabitha," Aidan said when we entered the house. His face was a twisted mess of pain and regret. He jumped from the wing chair in the living room and hesitantly came toward us. "I don't even know how to apologize for what has happened. This is all my fault, and I am so, so very sorry."

"Look, Aidan—"

"No, please, let me finish," he said as he held up his hand. Tabitha took a deep breath and crossed her arms, waiting. "I should never have lied to you. I should never have hidden who I was. My dishonesty and my fear of what Bobby would say lead in a direct line to your kidnapping. And I am so very sorry that you had to pay consequences for my choices."

"Are you done?" she asked him. He nodded.

"You lied to me, Charlotte lied to me, I lied to you. Bobby pretended to be a normal person and not a complete tool," Tabitha told our friend. "She was a witch and didn't tell me, you're...whatever the heck it is you are and no one told you. Life is full of secrets, dude," she shrugged. "I've mellowed a lot in the intervening year. I'm not mad anymore."

"I'm so glad," Aidan sighed with relief.

"Well, scratch that, I'm not mad about all of that secret stuff anymore," she said. "The fact that the two of you never bothered to call me, or write, or anything? That really ticks me off. Still. I know why Charlotte didn't contact me, but you were *here* for months longer. You knew that I called off my wedding because of how Bobby was treating you." She stepped forward. "How could you not contact me after that? How could you not call and see if I was okay?"

"I...I...I didn't think you would want to talk to me after what happened," Aidan stammered.

"You didn't *know*, though, did you?" Tabitha's accusation whipped at Aidan. My parents, Gunther's parents, and Devana slowly gathered around the outskirts of the room. "You didn't know because you didn't contact me. You were a coward. You left me alone to deal with my best friend disappearing, my fiancé being a jerk, with all these questions about what I knew and what I didn't know because *you* were a coward."

Kyle stepped forward to intercede between the two, but Aidan held his hand out to the side to stop his boyfriend from stepping in. Kyle's forehead furrowed as he stared at Tabitha, but he remained silent, just behind Aidan.

"You're right," he said. "I was a coward. I had

lost everything, and that's all I could think about. Since my lie caused you to lose everything, I assumed that you would hate me. But I never bothered to check. Since I never checked, I could never be there for you. It was selfish of me, and self-protective. And I am truly, truly sorry."

Tabitha stared at Aidan for a long time while the rest of us looked on. Her face was impassive, and if she was considering her former friend's words, none of us could tell by her expression. The moments ticked away. I held my own power in check, refusing to be an interloper on their exchange. I was afraid if I knew how they each were leaning, how Tabitha felt, that I would interfere and make it all worse.

This lie was originally my idea. That meant I bore some responsibility for the pain that came from it.

Just when I thought the tension could get no thicker, Tabitha shrugged and smiled at Aidan.

"Okay, that's done with," Tabitha said. She opened her arms wide and took two large strides forward to wrap her arms around Aidan. "I've missed you so much," she murmured. My eyes filled with tears when Tabitha extended her arm toward me and waved me into the group hug.

Rushing over, I wrapped the two tightly in my arms without thinking.

The howls of pain began almost immediately.

While we all sat in the living room reconnecting after the long absence, the door burst open and Tabitha's mother burst in. "Tabitha Stevens, I've been so worried about you!" she exclaimed. She raced across the space and headed directly for Tabitha. "Samantha told me that you were in the ritual room? Trapped as if you were an initiate! And without any training!"

"Mom, it was fine, really. Charlotte—" she began, and then her eyes met mine. I gave a subtle nod to my friend in the negative, not wanting her mother to know how Gunther and I had got her out. The woman clearly had a drinking problem, judging from our conversation previously. I didn't think it was a good idea for her to have details to babble the next time she became drunk in the wrong place. "Charlotte had been out near there looking for me, and she gave me a ride back," Tabitha told her mother.

"I never would've thought to look there,"

Samantha Goodfellow said as she waddled in the room. "Tabitha's very lucky that you had the forethought to look in that area."

"Why would you not have thought to look there?" I asked the high priestess, tilting my head in confusion. I realized for the first time that Samantha Goodfellow *should* have been the first person to recognize what Tabitha's car was in proximity of. "Didn't you realize when the news reported where Tabitha's abandoned car was found that it was right near your coven's ritual area?"

"It *was* right near the coven's ritual area," Samantha murmured. Sarah Stevens walked over to the chubby woman and wrapped an arm about her shoulder. "Sarah, why didn't we realize the car was right near the ritual area?" Samantha Goodfellow asked her coven member. Sarah reached her hand up and squeezed the back of Samantha's neck.

"Oh, old friend, you must be under so much stress after Raven told you what he did," Sarah said, squeezing. "Charlotte, have some understanding for the poor woman. We are only here because Raven came to find her to confess what he'd done. Imagine the *shock* the poor woman felt when she realized her son was responsible for kidnapping my daughter."

"Yes, I was quite shocked," Samantha nodded. Her eyes wandered around the room distractedly.

"Raven came to see you?" Tabitha asked.

"He did, he came to see me, he came home after he left the grotto," she nodded, her voice so low I had to strain to hear her. As Samantha's eyes met mine, it appeared her pupils were dilated. "Can I have some water, please? Suddenly, I'm so very thirsty." Sarah removed her hand as High Priestess Goodfellow shuffled unsteadily toward a chair.

"Are you all right, Ms. Goodfellow?" I asked. Reaching out with my power, I could feel the woman was calm but disoriented, and very tired.

"Yes, yes, Charlotte, I'm sure I'm just fine," she said as my mother handed her a glass of ice water. "It's just been a very stressful few days, I suppose, and I'm not a spring chicken anymore."

"Mrs. Stevens, do you know anything about what your husband, Darius, was planning?" I asked Tabitha's mother.

"Charlotte!" Tabitha snapped, and she shot me a look that made it clear she was not happy that I had mentioned her father's potential guilt in her disappearance. "Mom, Charlotte doesn't know that Dad's done anything for sure. It was just something that Raven said at the pool."

"Of *course* your father's done something, Tabitha," Sarah Stevens rolled her eyes at her daughter as she scratched a bright red, inflamed square patch of skin on her forearm. "There's never a time where your father *hasn't* done something."

Tabitha's eyes narrowed. "Mom, I don't want to do this here."

"I doubt there's a person in this room that doesn't believe your father is responsible for kidnapping you," Sarah Stevens shot back in a voice laced with steel. "You're the only one that still doesn't realize your father is a horrible man, and he deserves to go to jail."

"Mom, I *don't want to do this here*," Tabitha repeated, her voice steely and slow to match her mother's. I could feel the tension that had erupted between the two in just the last few seconds, a red-hot anger and resentment I didn't realize existed before this moment.

"*You always take his side*," Sarah snarled with such fury I jumped.

"Stop it," Tabitha said coldly.

The two women stared at one another as Aidan and I shared a surprised glance. I wasn't sure where the weak-willed, weepy, unsteady drunk woman went that we had spoken to, but Tabitha's mother was completely different in this room than we had thought she was.

*Charlotte, I hate to interrupt your thoughts,* Gunther said politely within my head. *But even I can sense the anger rising in this room. Considering that Darius and Raven may be on their way to the Magical Midway to steal something, I would suggest that we relocate this group onto the grounds so you have your full powers. I may not be able to focus on breaking up more than one fight,* Gunther pointed out as his eyes warily stared at mother and daughter.

*More than one fight?* I asked him.

*Once he steals whatever he is going to steal, what will happen then?* Gunther asked. *We don't know. He could come after you directly, or perhaps there's some human magic ritual he wants to perform. Either way, you're much more useful, and it's much safer for all of us if we go on the Magical Midway grounds, and we both have powers.*

I nodded, and Gunther took point on gathering the group and explaining what we were doing, leaving out the part regarding our concern that Tabitha and Sarah were about to come to blows in the living room. The entire time, Tabitha and Sarah Stevens held one another's eyes, their muscles straining as if they were holding themselves back from attacking one another.

# CHAPTER 14

"Okay, this is absolutely amazing." Tabitha walked around my yurt and marveled. Her mother watched her suspiciously from the couch next to Samantha Goodfellow, her gigantic Fendi bag resting on her lap as if it were a shield. The high priestess still seemed disoriented, her arms spread wide and her breath shallow. Sarah seemed unconcerned.

"It's just a yurt," I told her, shrugging. "We've had to make it bigger several times because we've picked up various people in our travels."

"Well, you were a professional straight animal grabber," Tabitha pointed out as we walked around the perimeter of the room. "Are these all just bedrooms or are they little apartment-like things, or what?"

"Here, let me show you." I pointed toward my door. "If you need to use the bathroom, you'll have to go in my bedroom, anyway. Each one of the bedrooms has a private bathroom, kind of like a hotel room. I didn't put one in the common room. It just seemed like a lot of bathrooms already."

"Yeah, I guess so," Tabitha said, counting the number of doors off the common area to herself.

As we pushed the door open, Samson's head rose from the bed. *You found your lost friend, I see.*

"You have a cat?" Tabitha asked, surprised. "I thought you were more of a dog person?"

Samson hissed, and Tabitha jumped.

"I do, and I am, kind of." I sat down on the bed and Samson leisurely pushed himself up on his feet and walked over with outward disinterest. "Samson is a bit of a special case for a cat."

"Holy crap, he's the circus familiar!" Tabitha yelped. Samson glared at her and his ears flexed forward toward her. "You know, I read in a book about the ringmaster familiars, but there was so little information about them I just dismissed it." She leaned down and stared into Samson's eyes.

He stared back. "I can't believe he's *real*. Can they really talk?"

"He can talk to me, telepathically," I told her. I reached out and caressed Samson's head. The cat began a low purr of contentment, though he never took his eyes from Tabitha. "It's kind of hard to explain, really. But he's definitely real, and he can definitely talk."

"That's just crazy," she murmured and extended her hand toward his face. He hissed again.

*Don't bite her*, I told Samson.

*I'm not going to bite her*, the cat retorted. *But she thinks I'm a fierce, omnipotent magical creature. Fierce, omnipotent magical creatures just don't roll over for scratches. You have to earn the attention of a fierce, omnipotent magical creature*, Samson explained with an ample infusion of arrogance in his thoughts. *She has not yet earned my attention.*

I sighed.

"What? He doesn't like me, does he? It is a male cat, right?" Tabitha's eyes glanced up at me, and then she tilted her head and tried to take a peek underneath Samson's belly.

Samson hissed again and lowered his body down closer to the bed to block her view. *Your*

*friend is remarkably rude. Remarkably rude.*
*Unbelievable.*

"Let's just say he likes himself more than anyone else, and he's choosy about who he shares himself with. He's not sure you earned it," I told her with a chuckle.

"Your life has *really* changed, Charlotte," Tabitha sighed. She pulled herself back from the defensive Samson. "When I started looking into where you might've gone, I was *completely* freaked out. Honestly, I thought something absolutely terrible *had* happened to you after I saw your father with the dogs." She climbed up on the bed and crossed her legs. Leaning her face on her hand, she sighed again.

"Seeing something like that when you don't know it can be done—I'm not ashamed to admit it *totally* freaked me out. But, you know, then I remembered it was your dad. After that, I put two and two together. I think it took me two weeks after *that* before I became completely jealous. This whole thing is just amazing."

"Two weeks?" I asked her, confused. "What do you mean, two weeks? Two weeks after you saw my dad with the dogs? Or two weeks after you found whatever information you found? Or..."

"Not sure what you mean," Tabitha said,

raising her eyebrow. "I *was* really worried about you and stuff. It took me a couple of months to process what I saw. My mom was actually a *really* big help in the beginning," Tabitha said. "When we came across the book that had the stories of the circuses in it? She changed. She got really tightlipped and closemouthed, and she even tried to convince me that all of it was bunk. I stopped working with her on it and went to Avalon Grove instead. It just got too *weird*."

"What do you mean, too weird?" I asked her. My pulse was racing. The more Tabitha told me about how she found this information, the more what I thought I knew didn't add up. According to Sarah Stevens, when Aidan and I went to visit her, Tabitha saw my father doing something unexplainable. That led Tabitha to believe something terrible had happened to me. Then when Aidan "disappeared," she thought something terrible happened to *him*.

That wasn't two weeks.

That wasn't even two months and two weeks.

"I don't know, my mom's always been...I don't even really know how to explain, Charlotte," Tabitha said, gesturing toward the door of my living area. "We don't really have a close family life. We never have. My mother's an alcoholic, my dad is incredibly cruel to her about it, but it's like this gigantic cycle that just keeps running around in the same circle over and over again. Dad's mean, Mom drinks, Mom screams at Dad, Dad's cold to Mom, Mom withdraws to her bedroom for days and weeks, and drinks. Dad's mean about it, and here we go again."

"Geez, Tabitha, I'm really sorry," I told her. I continued to pet the purring Samson. My comment seemed almost flippant, given what she just outlined, but I didn't know what else to say. What you say to someone that just happened to get crappy parents? "Why didn't you ever talk to me about what you were going through?"

"What was I supposed to say?" she smiled sadly. "I've had to cover for them all of my life. Cover for her drinking, cover for the fact that he seems to have no feelings about *anything* whatsoever. They are so wrapped up in what everybody else thinks of them that they made me a participant in the show they put on for the world. I *hated* it," she said through gritted teeth, the first flash of rage I had seen since we came in this room. After a few moments, it drained away forcefully and she was open and calm again. "I think it's why I was so mad at you and Aidan. I was just incensed that I couldn't get away from the dishonesty, the lies…I was afraid it would follow me all of my life."

I was mortified that something I did *just* to make my life a little bit easier (and to get Tabitha's constant, incessant harping that I find a man over with) had such deep emotional consequences for my friend. I was also embarrassed that I, one of the most powerful witches in the world and lifelong empath, never got out of my own selfish concerns long enough to see what should have been obvious.

*Especially* to me.

"If I had any idea, if I had known, Tabitha, I never would've lied to you. I never meant to hurt you, and I feel terrible that I did," I apologized again.

"I know you didn't. It took me a while to remember that, but I know you didn't," she smiled at me.

"So, I know we're having kind of a heartfelt moment here?" I squeezed Samson one last time and moved to push myself off the bed. "But I have to tell you—what you've just told me? It's not the story your mom told me at all."

"What did she tell you?" Tabitha asked, getting up. Nothing in her expression indicated any surprise, but her eyes narrowed.

"She told both me and Aidan that you were desperate to find us because you thought that there was evil in this town and it had taken us, or something. Like you had always been worried for a whole year that we were in trouble," I told her as we moved toward the door.

"She knew that I wasn't," Tabitha frowned. "Why would she say that? What am I saying?" Tabitha rolled her eyes and her pace toward the door picked up. "My mother lies the way most people breathe."

"Yes, but *why* did she lie?" I asked her.

The two of us headed back toward the common area to find out.

"All right, mom, what the heck is the deal?" Tabitha burst through my door into the living room. "Why did you tell Charlotte that I've been freaked out and worried about her since she left?"

I *probably* would've approached the situation with more finesse, but that clearly wasn't Tabitha's way. I tried to remember if it ever was, but…not really. Tabitha Stevens had always been a polite but direct type of gal. She reminded me a lot of Fiona, actually.

Okay, then. Let's get this party started, shall we?

Sarah Stevens' face was impassive as her daughter walked up on her. "I don't know *what* you're talking about," she mumbled and turned her face away. "I'm feeling somewhat faint from the stress of the past few days, Tabitha. Leave Mommy alone for now, please. We can talk about this some other time."

"Yes, yes, talk some other time," Samantha Goodfellow nodded, settled down even further into the couch cushions, and closed her eyes. "So tired, been a very stressful few days. Shouldn't talk to your mother that way, Tabitha."

"Samantha, you really need to butt out of this discussion," Tabitha told the sleepy high priestess. "This is between my mother and me, and she doesn't need your help."

"Don't talk to the coven high priestess like that!" Sarah Stevens snapped at her daughter. She leaned forward on the couch, suddenly alert. "I didn't raise you to speak to your elders like that."

"Oh, give it a rest, Mom," Tabitha said. She walked in front of her mother and sat down on the coffee table, facing her. "I asked you a question. Why did you tell Charlotte I've been worried about her since she left? You know darn well that we figured out where she was and who she was after a month of looking," Tabitha crossed her arms.

I watched the two of them.

"I had been drinking, Tabitha, I didn't know what I was saying," she told her daughter breathlessly, waving her hands in the air between them. "I'm sorry, I know Mommy shouldn't drink—"

"That's *not* going to work here," Tabitha told her.

"You know, Samantha Goodfellow told us that the two of you had a very close relationship," I told Tabitha. I walked over to the two women. "I have to tell you—I'm not really feeling it."

"We don't," my friend told me. "I'm about as suspicious of my mother as your cat Samson was of me when I tried to pet him over there." Tabitha hitched her thumb toward my bedroom area. "My mom is a master manipulator, Charlotte. She pretends not to be by blaming everything on the alcohol, but I've seen it enough times to know *exactly* who she is."

"I won't be spoken to in this manner!" Sarah Stevens stood up and grabbed her big Fendi purse, placing it between her and Tabitha. "I am your *mother*! You will treat me with *love and respect*!"

"I will when you *earn* it," Tabitha retorted.

Mother and daughter stared at one another in a stony silence that the rest of us feared to break.

"I need to go to the powder room," Sarah whispered angrily. She stepped to the side and walked toward my bedroom. Turning around, she stared at her angry daughter. "When I return to this room, I will expect you to treat me with the respect that I deserve as the person who brought you life. If you don't, if you can't, I will leave here, and you never have to see me again."

"Everything's gotta be high drama with you, doesn't it?" Tabitha rolled her eyes. "Just calm down, woman, and go empty your bladder."

My bedroom door slammed.

"Sorry about that, you guys," said my friend. She walked toward the wing chair situated as far away from my bedroom door as any place to sit could be in the room. "I wish she had just stayed home and stayed out of the situation so you wouldn't have to see that. Her drama just adds to the issue. That woman can't stand if *anyone* else is the center of attention."

"Yes," Samantha Goodfellow nodded sleepily. "Tabitha's right, Sarah has to be the center of

attention and her drama just adds to the issue."
The rotund woman yawned, grabbed a pillow,
and shoved it under her head. "Wish she had just
stayed home," High Priestess Goodfellow nodded.

Well, that was weird. Samantha Goodfellow
had gone from completely agreeing with Sarah
Stevens to completely agreeing with Tabitha
Stevens in the space of about five minutes. That
didn't make any sense, and my eyes narrowed as I
stared at her.

*Charlotte—*

*Hold on a second, Samson.*

*But Charlotte—*

*In a minute.*

"Is it just me, or is Samantha Goodfellow
acting completely weird?" I asked the group.

"Yes, it's just you. Samantha Goodfellow is
acting completely weird," the high priestess
murmured. She nodded yes and smiled in her
groggy state.

"She's agreeing with everything. Like,
*everything*," I told Tabitha. Across the room, Kyle
frowned and moved quickly to examine
Samantha Goodfellow. Aidan followed him.

"That *is* kind of weird," Tabitha said. "High
Priestess, are you all right? Have you been sick?"

"I'm all right," she nodded, smiling happily at Tabitha. "I've been sick."

The door to my bedroom opened, and an angry Sarah Stevens walked out. "Are you ready to give me the respect that I deserve, Tabitha Stevens?" Samantha snapped as she confronted her daughter.

"Mom, not now." Tabitha waved her away without pulling her eyes from Samantha Goodfellow. "We have a real issue here, not one of your manufactured dramas to make sure that everybody pays attention to you. The high priestess is acting weird. We're trying to make sure she's okay."

"That was your *last* chance, daughter," Tabitha's angry mother shouted. She wrapped her arms around her purse and hugged it. "You'll regret this. You'll *regret* not giving me the respect I *deserve* as your mother." With that pronouncement, Sarah Stevens turned deliberately on her heel and walked out of the yurt with a flourish.

As I watched her leave, something nagged at me.

∾

I cast a nervous glance at Tabitha.

"Oh, don't worry about her," my friend answered, jerking her thumb toward the closing front door. "That was just standard Sarah Stevens drama. With all the attention on me when I was kidnapped, her narcissistic cup must've got super drained. She'll be fine. Well, she'll still be her, but what you just saw is pretty much standard Mom."

*And I thought the ringmaster egos were bad,* Gunther thought.

"She's got some kind of patch on her neck," Kyle said as he tilted Samantha's head gently. "It's right behind her ear."

"What is it? A nicotine patch?" I asked.

"Samantha Goodfellow has never smoked a day in her life," Tabitha said. "What does it say on the patch?"

"Scopolamine," Kyle sounded out. "It's a drug that's—"

"Oh, wait, I heard of that!" Tabitha said, snapping.

"Me, too," Aidan said, his expression tightening. Then his eyes grew wide in shock. "It's used to treat motion sickness, but there's rumors that at really high levels it can be used to make people compliant as well as cause amnesia for a period of time."

"That's right, I saw that documentary! Supposedly people were spiking drinks with scopolamine in nightclubs and bars and then robbing them when the drug took effect," Tabitha nodded. "There was even a claim that somebody emptied their bank account for the robber because they were rendered so compliant by the drug."

"Where would someone get a drug like that?" I asked the group.

"Any doctor could prescribe it," Kyle said, shrugging. "There's nothing on the patch tells me whether this was prescribed for Samantha Goodfellow or not, though. It could be hers. She could just be having a reaction to it."

"No way," Tabitha shook her head and leaned forward to brush the hair from Samantha's face. Her brow furrowed with concern. "She's a high priestess and a dedicated homeopath. The only way she would take a modern pharmaceutical is if it was a matter of life or death, like chemotherapy for cancer or something. There's no way this woman would slap a drug that powerful on her skin on purpose. Not a chance. I'm telling you, that's not normal."

"Your world is very strange." Gunther watched the four of us fanned out around

Samantha Goodfellow. "I would suggest, however, that before you all continue discussing the ways in which your world is very strange that you consider removing the patch from behind the high priestess's neck. At least, do so if you are sure there is likely no good reason the thing is attached to her."

The four of us looked at one another, slightly embarrassed that none of us had thought of it. Tabitha waved toward Kyle, who was in the best position to do so.

"Oh, right," Kyle nodded, and leaned forward to carefully peel the two inch by two inch patch from behind the woman's thick neck. "Just give me a few more seconds, Ms. Goodfellow."

"I'll give you a few more seconds," she sighed happily as her chubby hand reached out and patted Kyle's thigh. "Such a handsome boy."

"There, done," Kyle said as he carefully held the very edge of the peeled off patch out toward Aidan, who was waiting with a plastic Ziploc bag to seal it up. "Be careful, don't let it touch your skin." Aidan nodded.

"Ms. Goodfellow, are you feeling any better?" I asked her. "Can you tell us why you were wearing that scopolamine patch?"

"I'm feeling better," she sighed dreamily and

leaned toward Kyle, who was still next to her with his hand on her back. "I could tell you."

"I don't think she's right about that," Kyle said. "I know a little bit about this drug from when our department was afraid it was going to start showing up as a date rape drug." He slowly lowered Ms. Goodfellow so she was lying sideways on the couch. "I would've told you all that I knew if you hadn't interrupted me to let me know you'd seen information about it on YouTube or whatever," he said sarcastically.

Man, was everyone's ego out of control tonight?

"She's going to be out of it for a while," Kyle continued. "Thing is, she shouldn't be, based on the dose written on that patch. Right now, I suspect the dose on the patch is not accurate. Either someone added more, or someone also gave her a shot at some point."

"Why would someone do that?" Tabitha asked.

"To make someone forget what they knew?" Kyle said. "To make someone compliant?"

"If what you say is true, though, someone would have to have more than a standard scopolamine prescription because they get nauseous on a boat," I said to Kyle. "I mean, to get someone that woozy," I pointed toward the happily snoring Samantha Goodfellow. "It would take a lot, right?"

"More than what comes on a single patch, yeah, I would think so," Kyle nodded.

"Darius Stevens works for a biomedical company," Aidan pointed out. "A biomedical company means drugs, right? Tabitha, do you know if your father has access to drugs like that?"

"Sure," she nodded. "He works in biomedical research with computer models and algorithms and stuff, but that's just a department. It's a pharmaceutical company, so yeah, of course they have tons of drugs all over the place."

"That's just one more clear indication that your Dad is at the center of this," Kyle said sadly. "Man, I'm really sorry. You really seem to have got the short stick in the parents' department."

"Yeah, maybe it was karma," she shrugged. "The universe had to balance out the fact that I would have unbelievably cool friends in my adulthood by giving me really, really crappy parents. A girl can't have a charmed life from beginning to end, you know."

"Excuse me, Ringmaster?" Bob, the lares guard, stuck his head in the front door of the yurt. I swiveled my head and waved him in. "I don't mean to bother you, or anything, or, like, your guest who's clearly enjoying an awesome nap." Bob gestured toward Samantha Goodfellow. "But we've been patrolling and we haven't really found anything out of sorts except, like, one itty-bitty thing. Just one. Not a big deal. But wanted to ask you about it."

"Shoot," I told him.

"Um. I don't have my bow and arrow." Bob scratched his head, a look of confusion playing across his features. "I could, like, go get it if you want." Tabitha snorted at Bob's response, and his confusion was quickly replaced by a wide smile and batting eyes.

Oh, you have to be kidding me.

"No, Bob, I mean ask your question."

Bob and Tabitha stared at each other, giggling.

"Bob!"

"Right, boss! No need to shout." He whirled around and faced me. "When that lady left, though, I heard a cat screeching like its tail was on fire—"

I blinked, and all the little things added up.

*Her parents knew where she was*, Raven said in the grotto.

*I was just incensed that I couldn't get away from the dishonesty, the lies*, Tabitha told me about her family life. Her mother specifically. Her manipulative mother.

Mrs. Stevens shock when she burst into my house, that Tabitha had been found in the ritual room.

Mrs. Stevens going to the bathroom. My bathroom. Off my bedroom.

Without asking where it was.

My stomach dropped.

I could have called out telepathically to Samson. It would've been the logical thing to do, to check and see if he was still on the property. To give him a chance to respond from his normal perch on the bed, curled up on my pillow and shedding away so his black hairs invaded my nose as I slept.

But I knew.

My mind cast back to the gigantic bag Sarah Stevens clutched as she stormed out of the yurt.

I knew.

I didn't have to check.

I could feel his absence, could feel he was no longer on the fairgrounds. It was like missing the other side of myself, an absence I had been too busy to notice.

Now that I had, though, it was all I could think about and all I could feel.

All at once, memories raced through my mind and observations continued to snap into place. The first night I became ringmaster and Samson's claws raking along my legs to draw blood. The protections that the Magical Midway wrapped around me to ensure my skin could never be broken by any weapon. That something needed to be stolen, my blood alone wasn't enough, from the Magical Midway to...to...

"It's been Sarah Stevens all along," I whispered, heartbroken.

Sarah Stevens had stolen Samson as I sat oblivious in the next room. My familiar had called out to me, and I pushed him off. Ignored him, really.

I had missed the signs, even the ones people tried to shove in my face.

And if we didn't stop her, she would steal the Magical Midway next.

THANK YOU FOR READING!

I hope you enjoyed A Call to Charms! Charlotte's adventures continue in Book 7, Hole Lotta Magic!

# KEEP UP WITH LEANNE LEEDS

Thanks so much for reading! I hope you liked it! Want to keep up with me?

Visit leanneleeds.com to:

Find all my books...

Sign up for my newsletter...

Like me on Facebook...

Follow me on Twitter...

Follow me on Instagram...

Thanks again for reading!

Leanne Leeds

# FIND A TYPO?
# LET US KNOW!

Typos happen. It's sad, but true.

Though we go over the manuscript multiple times, have editors, have beta readers, and advance readers it's inevitable that determined typos and mistakes sometimes find their way into a published book.

Did you find one? If you did, think about reporting it on leanneleeds.com so we can get it corrected.